Staff

Founder and Executive Editor Meredith Allard

Deputy Editor Susan Arenstein

Senior Editor Paula Day

Contributors

Briana Beebe
Matthias Berger
Peter Bridges
Jonathan Chan
Rosanne Dingli
Deborah H. Doolittle
David Mampel
Richard Elliott Martin
Ayden McLane
Peter D. McQuade
W. Barrett Munn
Jennifer O'Neill Pickering
Sue Petty
Mary Elizabeth Pope
Sally R. Rae
Albert Schlaht
Jennie Treverton

EDITORIAL OFFICE
2654 W. Horizon Ridge Pkwy
Suite B5-364
Henderson, NV 89052

For advertising, contact:
copperfieldreview@gmail.com

For submission guidelines:
www.copperfieldreviewquarterly.com

ISSN: 1533-3736

Cover Photo Credit:
Justin Kauffman

Contents Photo Credit:
Marcos Paulo Prado

www.copperfieldreviewquarterly.com
www.copperfieldreview.com.
Copperfield Press LLC

WINTER 2022

COPPERFIELD
REVIEW
QUARTERLY

CONTENTS

DEAR READERS

How has your start to 2022 been?

With the endless waves of COVID, as well as a hearing test that revealed that whatever little hearing I might have had is fading away, I admit that I've been floundering a bit. Normally, after my winter hiatus, I'm raring to get back to editing *Copperfield* and completing my own writing projects. That sense of raring to go hasn't happened to me yet in 2022. Work is getting done, but I feel like I'm slogging through mud, going backward, or both.

I know from writer friends that they're feeling the same. We're beginning yet one more year in a state of uncertainty. But instead of dwelling on the negativity, I'm learning to focus on the positive. I'm focusing on what it means to live a writer's life because that is where I find the most meaning.

So what, then, is a writer's life?

A writer's life is making a commitment to putting words on paper, whether by hand or on a keyboard. It means staying in close contact with the storyteller inside you. It means being attuned to the inspiration all around you. It means rediscovering your inner child—the one who loved to play make-believe, dress in costumes, and create new worlds under homemade tents. It means remembering the activities you loved when you were younger and probably still do deep down somewhere.

A writer's life means freely admitting our love of language and rhythm and meaning. A writer's life is born from a love of words, first words found in other people's short stories and books and later our own words in our own short stories and books. A writer's life means seeking beauty in the mundane. For some of us, writing is our calling, so living a writer's life means discovering that calling and staying true to it despite the myriad of challenges. A writer's life means being creative, sharing the truest part of yourself, and letting your soul roam free. For many of us, myself included, writing is a way to say things we can't say any other way.

Really what I'm talking about is authentic living, which means living in a way that's true to who you are deep down inside. If you're a writer, it means living in a way that honors the writer in you.

There's a wonderful post about authentic living on postivepsychology.com. Here's some of what they say about engaging in authentic living:

"Listen to your inner voice rather than losing it in the noise of others'. Make it an ongoing process to listen to your hopes, dreams, and fears.

Know yourself, what you are good at, what you are prepared to do, and what you are not.

Face up to the truths of who you are. Honesty is not always pleasant, but it has the potential to free you.

Own yourself and your truths. Don't let others push you into their way of thinking, but also don't stick to views when you are proved wrong or they no longer work for you.

Take responsibility for your choices.

Be yourself; be honest and transparent in your dealings. People like and are drawn to those they perceive as sincere and genuine and distrust those who are not."

to Credit: Donnie Rosie

Easier said than done, right? Living an authentic life, which for me means living a writer's life, is a challenge, yes, but it's one I'm ready for.

In moments of contemplation brought on by COVID and other ordeals, I realized that I had lost the joy of writing. I had forgotten how much fun it is to write a story for the story's sake. I mourned the loss of that joy and I wondered how I could get it back. Because, really, what is the point of writing if you don't enjoy it? There are so many other ways to spend your time or make a living. I wrote this post about how I had nearly given up writing for good.

I'm in the process of reclaiming that joy by making a conscious attempt to seek it. If you've read Writing Down the Bones by Natalie Goldberg then you're familiar with the concept of Beginner's Mind. Here's a wonderful definition of Beginner's Mind from Leo Babauta from Zen Habits:

"It's dropping our expectations and preconceived ideas about something, and seeing things with an open mind, fresh eyes, just like a beginner. If you've ever learned something new, you can remember what that's like: you're probably confused, because you don't know how to do whatever you're learning, but you're also looking at everything as if it's brand new, perhaps with curiosity and wonder."

That's it exactly. I had lost my curiosity and wonder about writing.

One of the ways I've been dealing with my lost curiosity and wonder is by consciously pursuing a writer's life. A writer's life takes work, though. It requires persistence. I have to take time every day to look for things that bring me joy, including writing. It means practicing gratitude, which I've been particularly terrible at lately. The myriad of problems we're dealing with, while not unprecedented in history, are unprecedented to us. As humans, we have an innate fear of the unknown, and we've been living in a constant state of unknowns for two years.

These days I've settled into a mild null with the acceptance that things are in constant flux and they will be for some time. That concession has opened enough headspace that I could begin looking honestly at my writing and my life and I wasn't entirely happy with what I saw. Something had to give, and the easiest thing for me to change was my outlook. I made the decision to live deliberately. As Thoreau said,

"I went to the woods because I wished to live deliberately, to front only the essential facts of life, and see if I could not learn what it had to teach, and not, when I came to die, discover that I had not lived. I did not wish to live what was not life, living is so dear; nor did I wish to practice resignation, unless it was quite necessary. I wanted to live deep and suck out all the marrow of life…"

For me, living deliberately includes making a special place in my heart for writing. Not writing because I have to. Writing because I want to. Because it is an authentic part of who I am. Because it brings me joy. And yes, that includes the physical act of writing—sitting my bottom into the chair and dancing my fingers across the keyboard, typing out words that become sentences that in time become stories.

When everything else in my life fails me, even in the depth of the darkest days of a pandemic we are not yet through, writing saves me. Even the healing that has come from writing this, which has been on my mind for some time, is palpable.

Whether you love to write, or if you have some other creative endeavor that lights you up from the inside out, your time may feel much fuller when you make a deliberate attempt to include the magic of creativity into your daily life. Living deliberately means different things to different people. What does it mean to you?

I hope that you are able to find the joy that is in your life, right there, now, today.

Meredith

Meredith Allard
Executive Editor, *Copperfield Review Quarterly*

IT'S NEVER TOO LATE TO BEGIN

AN INTERVIEW WITH MARY RESSENOR

By Meredith Allard

Mary Ressenor is the author of the Victorian time-travel fantasy *A Question of Time*. Mary talks about her experience writing her first novel at the age of 65 and how once she started writing she never looked back. She lives in Portland, Oregon.

Meredith Allard: Tell our readers a little bit about yourself and your journey toward becoming a writer.

Mary Ressenor: Oh goodness! Where to begin? Like many writers, I began as a reader. I loved reading through school. I thought of becoming a writer in college, but I ended up marrying my college sweetheart and we had three beautiful children together. My dream of writing was put on the back burner while I raised my children. I also worked part-time as a school librarian, which I loved a lot. It's a great feeling to introduce young children to favorite books and authors.

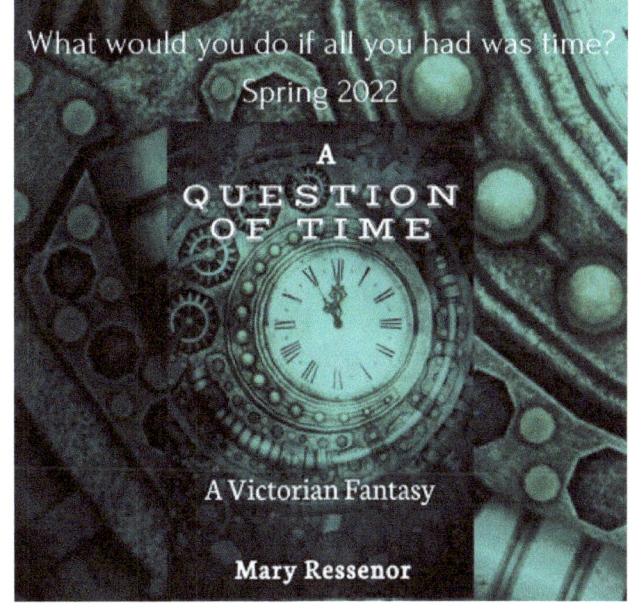

When I was in my 60s my husband died suddenly and it was devastating. On the outside, I held myself together for my children and grandchildren, but inside I was falling apart. My therapist recommended journaling as a way to help me work through my feelings about my husband's death, and I did find journaling very therapeutic.

I kept a journal for several years before I realized that I was writing about more than my feelings. I was writing down snippets of conversations I had overhead and story ideas. It was the beginning of my writer's notebook. In time, that notebook was filled with character sketches, conversations, and plot diagrams. I realized that I had a story that I had to tell.

After I retired from my librarian's job I finally settled myself to writing this story as a full-length novel.

M.A.: Did you always intend to write historical fiction?

M.R.: I have very eclectic tastes as a reader. I love everything from romance to fantasy to time travel. I also love history. Lately, I've been reading historical fiction exclusively, especially historical fiction about the Victorian age. My daughter is an avid reader of time travel novels, and when she first told me about that genre I thought thanks but no thanks. It didn't sound like something I'd be interested in.

But when she insisted I read some of her favorite time travels books, I loved them. I loved that the fantasy story was inspired by history. As I started thinking about the novel I wanted to write, I realized that the Victorian era was part of the story, but I also realized that there would be fantasy and time travel and even some steampunk influence. I love that when I write fiction I can create the world in my own way. There are no limits!

M.A.: Did learning how to write come easily for you?

M.R.: I think because I finally settled myself down to writing at the age of 65 I came into the experience with an open mind. I have enough life experience behind me to know that nothing comes easily and everything worthwhile takes time to learn.

I took both in-person and online creative writing courses. I wrote every chance I had. It was easier because I was retired by this point so I was free to spend my days writing. But I wasn't going to rush into anything. I made the decision that the book would take as long as it would take. When the book is released this year it will be three years since I started writing it. I wouldn't trade any bit of those three years because I learned so much during that time.

M.A.: As an editor, I've encountered many would-be writers who tell me that they feel like they've missed out on their chance to begin writing because they didn't start young enough. One of the things I love about your story is that you're living proof that that isn't true.

M.R.: Yes! I've had friends my own age say to me, oh, I'd love to do what you're doing but I missed the boat. I want to tell them, and everyone else, that it's never too late to pursue your dreams. Elizabeth Gilbert in *Big Magic* talks about how you can never age out of writing the way you might with dancing or something like that, although I'd bet you money that there are plenty of dancers, actors, and models who got their start later in life. It's all about being brave enough to try.

Sometimes things may not work out the way you hoped but that doesn't mean it wasn't a valuable experience. There's a quote that's attributed to George Eliot: "It's never too late to be what you might have been." I have that quote taped to the wall behind my desk so it's the first thing I see when I turn on my computer every day.

I think you can only get better as a writer as you get older because you have more life experience behind you. I bet if you look at your favorite authors, I think you'll see that many of them are in their 60s, 70s, and beyond. So if you want to write, write. If you're 95, who cares? You're 95 anyway. You might as well be 95 and doing what you love.

M.A.: From your mouth, Mary...

All authors have a different path as they seek publication. What was your journey to publication like?

M.R.: Like most people of a certain age, I had my heart set on traditional publishing because that's all that was available for most of my life. I began the querying process with *A Question of Time*, and like most writers, I found the experience draining and disheartening.

I'd query one agent and they'd say no one wanted to read time travel fantasies anymore. Another agent would say that there are too many time travel stories out there. Plus, I had been reading a lot about agents that made me question if I needed one. I know not all agents are created equal, and there are some fabulous agents out there, but I thought I might be better off doing my own legwork.

I kept hearing about independent publishing, and the more I looked into it the more I thought it was an option for me. Yes, I have to handle everything myself, but I don't have to wait for a gatekeeper to give me permission to write the books I want to write.

Since *A Question of Time* is multi-genre, it's hard to place in an easy slot for agents and publishers. I think with work like that you're better off publishing independently. It's a lot of work to publish independently, but I also have a lot more control than I would have otherwise.

M.A.: It goes back to never being too old to learn new skills.

M.R.: That's right. I'm still learning. I'm learning about how to put together social media profiles and I'm learning how to put together my own website. I'm starting from scratch since I never used social media before. Right now I'm looking into Instagram because I love to take photographs. Some parts of learning to use social media are taking longer than others, but that's okay. I'm in this for the long haul and I have time to learn.

M.A.: What are the joys/challenges of writing historical fiction for you?

M.R.: I've always loved history, the Victorian era precisely, so I love delving into that world in detail. I wouldn't say there was much of a challenge because once I started writing historical fiction I found it so much fun I wondered why I didn't start sooner. I've never looked back! I love writing historical fiction with some fantasy thrown in and I'd never write anything else.

M.A.: What authors have inspired you in your writing and/or your own life?

M.R.: Just too many to name, really. Lately, I've been reading historical fiction exclusively, though some of my all-time favorites are Jane Austen, George Eliot, Edith Wharton, Willa Cather, and Margaret Atwood. I don't have a similar style to them and I don't try to write like them, but it was loving their books that made me want to write my own.

M.A.: What advice do you have for anyone who wants to begin writing at any age?

M.R.: Go for it! If we've learned anything from the coronavirus epidemic, it's that we're all on borrowed time on this earth. It's up to us to decide how we're going to spend that time.

For years, I wanted to write but I had a lot of reasons why I didn't. It wasn't until I was in my 60s that I finally allowed myself to try and I'm so glad I took the plunge.

No matter how old you are, take your time. Good writers aren't born that way. It takes a lot of practice to gain the skills you need to become a good writer. I've been writing for a few years now and I'm still learning something new every day. Take classes whether they're in person or online. Join writing groups. I have a wonderful group of friends that I meet for coffee once a week and we share what we're writing. Their feedback has been so valuable to me.

No matter how old you are, never stop learning. For me, that meant learning how to tell stories and learning how to use technology like social media and different websites. It's stagnating that makes you grow old.

If you want to be a writer, pick up that pen or open that keyboard and start putting words on the page. You can do what I did and simply start a journal since there's no pressure in a journal. Then if you have an idea for a short story or a novel, find those tools that will help you bring your dream to life. Life is too short to wish you were doing something you're capable of doing right now.

WHO ARE YOUR FAVORITE HISTORICAL FICTION AUTHORS?

BY MATTHIAS BERGER

Those of us who love to read historical fiction have our go-to authors whose novels we snap up as soon as we see that their latest book is published. Many of us are signed up for new release alerts from Amazon or BookBub for our favorite historical authors.

Who are your favorite historical fiction authors? Here's what *Copperfield's* readers and contributors had to say.

Mary Ressenor: I adore Diana Gabaldon's *Outlander* series. I love the time travel element and I love learning about Scottish history. Gabaldon spins a great yarn but she's also a good writer.

Jennifer Smythe: Hilary Mantel without a doubt. I've never read anything as enthralling as her books about Thomas Cromwell and Henry VIII. I'm reading her historical novel about the French Revolution now and it's wonderful.

Edwina: Even though his books are a bit dated, I still like John Jakes's novels about American history. I've been on a quest to read all of his historical novels and they're keeping me busy but in a good way.

Jessie B.: I'm a big fan of any historical novel written by Jennifer Chiaverini. She writes across different eras with books such as *Mrs. Lincoln's Dressmaker* and *The Women's March* and she pulls you back in time so that you feel like you're there.

Emily Marchand: Susan Vreeland by far. I was an art major in college and I love how she takes these masterpiece works of art and weaves a whole world around them.

Rebecca J.: Kate Quinn is a favorite. I love her Ancient Rome novels, but I'm starting to read her World War II fiction and I like those as well.

Albert Thurston: I've been reading Bernard Cornwell for years and I've enjoyed nearly everything I've read. I particularly like his Saxon books. I also love Wilbur Smith's novels about Ancient Egypt.

Martha Wilcox: I've been reading a lot of Mimi Matthews lately. Her books are Victorian and Regency romances and they're good for when you want something light and simple that is pure escapism.

Christopher C.: Ken Follett's *Pillars of the Earth* series is one of the best I've ever read. It's one of those series where you wish there were ten more books. I'll read any historical novel by Follett.

Antoinette: I love Marie Benedict's books about women in history may have been forgotten but who were important nonetheless. My favorite is *The Other Einstein*.

Janetta J.: Colson Whitehead has written some wonderful historical fiction that illuminates the experiences of Black people throughout history. Some of Toni Morrison's novels were also historical fiction, like *Beloved*, and her work always stands out as among the best of the best.

Brittney Johns: Isabel Allende's historical fiction is always a favorite. She has a way of bringing to life important stories from the past.

Charley Spencer: I'm probably showing my age here, but I love James Michener's epic historical sagas like *The Bridges at Toko-Ri*, *Hawaii*, and *Centennial*. They don't write epics like that anymore.

Celia: I think Madeline Miller's books based on Ancient Greek myths such as *The Song of Achilles* and *Circe* are wonderful. They give insight into the era while staying true to the stories we know.

HISTORICAL FICTION

ROSANNE DINGLI

DAVID MAMPEL

AYDEN MCLANE

PETER D. MCQUADE

SUE PETTY

MARY ELIZABETH POPE

JENNIE TREVERTON

THE PORTOLAN CHART OF 1557
By Rosanne Dingli

On the second Sunday, Jerónimo Jagus opened the box. Its key, on sweaty discoloured ribbon, was always around his neck, tucked inside his shirt, invisible to any others on board. The only other man who knew he had it was Puck.

The key had a small head. He struggled to turn it in the lock on the big box, grunted under his breath and remembered Mariolina swore by a bit of grease to lubricate stubborn mechanisms. He looked at the plate he had pushed away uneaten only a minute ago. The meat had turned before it was cooked. The lump of pork was nearly green, and he could hardly stomach the rice, in which small wrinkled raisins looked like ticks without blood; ticks picked off the carcass of some sick dog. If they did not reach a port within the next few days, and if those hands on the forward deck caught nothing, he would have a mutiny on his hands.

Mutiny caused by hunger and scabies was never a good prospect.

He scraped the small key over the greasy chop, looked at the smear of rucked lard it picked up, and inserted it into the lock once more, working it this way and that until he felt some give. It was only a few seconds until the lock opened with a small click.

Lying inside was his gold earring, which he never wore on board for fear of tempting fate. It was supposed to pay for his funeral, for which he was far from ready. The fear of his limp dead body being plunged into the sea in a grimy shroud lived with him, day and night. He wanted a land burial, but not for many years yet.

Next to the earring lay an exotic unguent-stained kerchief which still held the faint scent of Mariolina. It was embroidered with green thread someone had given her, someone off another ship, who had perished in the gales the year of the *sestiere* fires. His district was always under threat of fire. Ah, Mariolina; she was such a mystery. So much more sophisticated and cultured than he was. He failed to see what she saw in him, but his heart told him not to examine such sentiments too closely.

Under the silk kerchief, El Libro de Oracion Comun, his Book of Common Prayer, and underneath it, a folded chart. The chart was the whole reason behind this voyage. Onto it, he copied lines, drawings and descriptions from the sketches he made, hoping that mistakes and inaccuracies were confined to his scribbled pieces of paper and parchment, leaving this clean copy legible and unambiguous. For the little he discovered, he hoped to receive more than just praise. It was folded quite neatly, despite his disappointment and frustration.

'Some maps require folding, Jerónimo. Rolling such a map makes it awkward, vulnerable to tearing at the edges, and hard to handle. A folded map might have creases in crucial places, but it's easy to store and hide, and there is predictability in it.'

'And predictability...?'

'... gives you thinking time. Time to plan. Which is why you must always have a navigator who can figure and compensate for confusing paper folds, and who not only understands the weather, son, but feels it.' He was not about to let Carlos the navigator near this folded chart, but it was worth listening to advice from Rodolfo. His bosun Rodolfo, who despite all the tribulations of the voyage, had kept him steady and on course; who despite the loss of their companion ship, *Pasqualina*, had injected hope into his desperate mind.

"He would not show this map to Carlos; that would be complete folly. He regularly bent, peered, and argued with the craggy old man – who stabbed dirty fingers on everything – over another working chart, prepared for them in Venice.

Jerónimo had felt calm and reassured at the bosun's words. 'The Doge sent out two ships, Rodolfo. What is to become of us without a companion vessel?'

'We know nothing.' Rodolfo crossed himself, and crossed himself again. 'Only God knows if the Pasqualina is still afloat, and her men all safe. We have no idea. They might be alive and fearing for ...'

Jagus inhaled sharply. Rodolfo was right. 'Fear, fear, fear ... They might think that we are lost!'

The older man placed a hand on his chest. 'Exactly. They might be right at this instant thinking that we, the vessel with the only divers on board, with the only swimmers ...' He made a face. It was a rare sailor who was not afraid of the unknown creatures and perils of the sea. '... with the only possibility of assessing the true worth of whatever coastal land we find, have found the bottom, and have breathed our last.'

'And so they return to the east.'

'With all the peril that comes to a solitary vessel when that becomes necessary. Turning back to the east ...' He shivered. 'There exists no navigator, no commander, as you well know, sir, who will take the decision to turn east to a leeward course lightly, without great consideration and weighing of risks. It is ...' he lowered his voice an octave, '... both murder and suicide. Like I said, one's navigator must know the winds, the weather, and more. It is nothing short of crazy to turn east towards a landmass with the wind behind you.'

His navigator Carlos had arthritis in every joint, which foretold gales and calms like nothing else could. Carlos feared certain winds because of the pain they bore him, more than the sailing hazards they brought the *Carolina*. But having people like Carlos and Rodolfo around him compensated for the dull-witted lazy men that were inevitable last-minute additions to his thin crew. Carlos would never do what Rodolfo just described as insane.

Now, his hand trembled as he raised the map, unfolded it, and smoothed it out on the table. He looked at the stateroom door. Locked minutes before, it kept navigator, bosun, and first mate–the only ones with permission to come below to the forward stateroom–from entering. He looked at that door twice with his signature squint. It stayed shut.

His bad eye scared everyone on board when they caught its darkness, and recognized within it the glint of dogged purpose. Determination and perseverance to get whatever he wanted, no matter how long it took, how much dread it inflicted, or who had to die on his ruthless path towards it.

They had lost one man to a mouth infection just after broaching the Atlantic, another to a vicious deck brawl, and another who was struck dead on his feet by a swinging fore boom that got him on the back of the head. Throwing their poor bodies overboard was no mean undertaking. He was the one who had to say the prayer, the one who had to account to the Doge, and to God.

'It's Sunday, Lord.' He whispered under his breath, rumbling words through a dry throat. 'It's Sunday, the second Sunday since the storm, since the last sighting of *Pasqualina* and her commander, my good friend Angelicus. But You will perhaps forgive me a spot of study. We might be furlongs and fathoms away from our destination, but our general direction troubles me.' He ran a hand over his head. 'Not to speak of our present location.'

Each corner was weighted, each stained map corner had been held down through the months by cups of wine and sangria, plates of bread, and bowls of crunchy fried whitebait. Jagus weighted down corners of maps as a matter of course. This one was written and drawn on inferior parchment, but did not roll in upon itself, and was comparatively new, if stained and scribbled, but he did it anyway. It was what one did with maps and charts.

Today, it was his plate of discarded pork, a small brass compass in its worn case, and an eyeglass. The fourth corner was anchored by the heel of his left hand. A rumble started in the pit of his stomach. With a calloused finger, Jerónimo followed a line in purplish ink, one he had traced himself, which Rodolfo would have scolded him for; so roundly, so raucously would he have uttered, that the men on deck would have wondered what kind of disaster was about to descend upon them. 'Never write on a map! Arrghh!'

'It's a chart.'

'Arrghh! That's not the point.' How many times did the man make that point?

Jerónimo's hand trembled a little. He did not say aloud it was a portolan, made for writing on. He had never liked to gainsay Rodolfo.

'All charts are maps ... but not all maps are charts!' He could hear him in his head. 'Charts are navigational. They are made explicitly for those who sail. It's confusing and dangerous to add too many lines. I've said this many times. Jerónimo ... are you listening to me?' He had always listened to Rodolfo.

Rodolfo, who was wrapped in a shroud one deck below; a shroud stained with his brown blood, the little that could still trickle from him two hours after he found his inert form, lying in his cabin. His ears, bloodied and mangled, were thrown on the boards near his boots. 'Lord, you gave me a problem, for which I bow in humility and accept.' His eye twitched. 'But it was delivered to settle on a big pile of other problems.' His good eye roved and looked toward the wooden beams above his head. 'I would have appreciated it if You had waited for me to solve at least one of the other disasters on my hands.' He scratched the grizzled unshaved chin, whose cleft Mariolina liked so much. 'Perhaps I sound ungrateful and a wretch, but all I ask for is time, Lord. Some time, this blessed Sunday. That, or a sighting of *Pasqualina*. That, or a decent catch by those useless boys.'

Did his ears fool him or did he hear a cry above his head? Yes. No.

'Land ho!'

'Land ho!'

'Land!'

Land? Were they all losing their minds? Were hunger and idleness getting to all of them up there? A quick rap at his door made him hang his head in exasperation. 'Puck, I thought I told you...'

'Land, *Capitán*. You need to see this. Carlos asks you to kindly come above.'

'If you drag me up there to see a speck of uninhabited rock on the horizon, Puck, I'll have your guts for block ties.'

'Sir. You'd better come up, sir.'

The deck was crowded with all hands, all men, every living soul. Every living soul; Jerónimo winced. Everyone except Rodolfo, who had fallen foul of some vicious deck scramble. The men were turning rabid and mutinous. The shouts were loud. They had seen land before; what was all the fuss?

'What's all the fuss, Carlos?'

Emaciated, grim but focussed, the man in a striped knitted cap remained silent. His eyes were glued to the forward deck.

It was not only the sighting that had got them. The boys at the bow had hauled up a net that writhed with all manner of sea creature. It bulged with fish and rained seawater all over the deck.

'Sir!'

'Master!'

'Mister Jagus, sir!'

'*Capitán.*'

'Commander!'

'*Capitano!*

They called from every single spot on deck. It was bedlam, and he was right in the middle of it.

Jagus looked around, spooked by the waves and how the disturbed surface changed the colour of the water frequently, and in a strange way. It was green. No, blue, and then grey. And then golden, as shafts of light bounced off the rippled surface; plates of gold. And then such a deep blue it made him take a step back, experienced and worldly though he was. It was unearthly.

'So what have you there? A bucket of sculpin?' He laughed his hoarse laugh. It was incredible. An island on the horizon, all the sea colours in the world in one spot, and a forward deck ankle-deep in fish.

'Sculpin?' Puck was at his elbow. 'No sculpin here. Look at it, silver, big and beautiful fish. Not a bottom dweller among this haul. We shall eat well for days.'

'Tell Murg to prepare his pots and pans and barrels of salt. Tell him to throw out the last of the pork. And bring me my spyglass, Puck.'

'You came up without it, sir? You did – because you did not believe the call of land.' There was an accusation in the polite observation.

'Puck!'

'Yessir.' The first mate turned and disappeared down the first hatch. His head popped out for an instant, just long enough to bark an order at two men to mind the mizzen. And to catch a bleak look from his master's only seeing eye.

Without turning, Jerónimo took the spyglass from the breathless man who returned from below and held it to his eye. Incredible though it was, the men were right, and the excitement whose noise was still in his ears was warranted.

'Circum, Puck.'

'Yes, *Capitán* – we shall sail right around. And naturally, we seek …Both eyes were squeezed shut for a long moment. Barrel chest heaved with a laboured sigh. 'You have been a mariner as long as I, Puck. You know very well we seek a shore, a good leeward anchorage. A place to land, such as a beach of sand or shale or pebbles, even...'

'*Pietre nere.*'

'*Black pebbles*–what are you, Sicilian? We want a place where we can look for water, wood...'

'And women.'

Jerónimo aimed a wild kick at his mate's shins. 'Get out of here.' But it was he who moved. On his way, he avoided Carlos and his moth-eaten striped cap and distanced gaze as adroitly as the navigator avoided him. He had left the good map on the table below, and he had just remembered what a foolish thing it was to become forgetful and negligent with such a scurvy crew on board.

He rattled down the companionway and threw the spyglass on the table where his plate of greasy pork and the gleaming flat disc of the compass still lay.

An oath started in his belly and made its way to his throat. It trumpeted out of his stomach and chest, past a voice box that could still bellow with youthful lustiness. It reached the boys on deck who ignored it. They joyfully sorted through the catch and had no mind for the exclamations of their easily angered captain. They had no notion of what had happened in that brief interval he had shown himself above.

'Holy Mother of God!' Jerónimo slapped a hand on the old grey timber of his cabin table. His precious diagram, his most valuable piece of parchment, everything this voyage was about, had disappeared. The portolan chart was gone.

* * *

Rosanne Dingli has authored ten novels, six collections of awarded and published short stories, a handful of novellas, and a book of poetry. This excerpt is from *The Cartographer of Venice*, her ninth novel. Her themes are largely taken from the arts, literature, architecture, painting, music, and history. She has held a number of roles in publishing and has lectured in Creative Writing. She lives and writes in Western Australia.

Whispers of the Holy Spirit

By David Mampel

Montsegur, South of Paris, 1205.

"Esclarmonde!" Lord Pereille shouted in the ruins of the castle keep. "Come quickly! I have discovered something hidden near the cornerstone." Lord Pereille carefully put a metal box down on a large stone. Esclarmonde clambered over stones and bushes until she stopped in front of him. Lord Pereille looked at her with fire in his eyes. They stared in awe at the rectangular box about the size of a large book. Lord Pereille dusted off the top of the box, and two Ancient Greek letters appeared. "I can't read Greek, but I think these two letters are Alpha and Omega, the first and last letters of the Greek alphabet." Dusting off the entire box, he pulled out a leather-bound book with five additional Greek letters embossed on the front cover.

"I wonder what these five letters mean?" Esclarmonde shot a glance to Lord Pereille. "Do you know Ancient Greek? Wait! I remember Papa Nicetas once told me he had a dream that one day I would find...Heavens! This must be the lost book of Mary Magdalene's account of Jesus after he died!" Lord Pereille's eyes narrowed.

"My God!" Lord Pereille exclaimed. "We must search for a scholar in Toulouse."

"We must be careful though," Esclarmonde uttered. "We must find someone we can trust." Lord Perielle nodded. Esclarmonde placed her palm on the sacred book.

"Blessed wisdom," she said. "We give thee thanks for revealing your way of righteousness."

* * *

South of Paris. Foix, Occitania. 1209

Before the sun rose above the Pyrenees Mountains, Esclarmonde de Foix gasped and bolted upright at the sound of her brother's voice outside her chamber door. "Some may simply fight to the death," she heard her brother, Roger say. "This is our homeland. A true Occitain would rather die than be occupied by the North and the Papacy."

Clutching the bed coverings, she waited for her breathing to settle. Turning her head toward the fogged amber windows, her eyes widened when she realized the red glow on the distant clouds were from burnings at Beziers. Throwing off her blankets, she slipped into her smock and ran down the hall to her sister-in-law's chambers. Letting herself in, Esclarmonde roused Philippa from sleep.

"Esclarmonde! What is it?" Philippa tossed back her blankets and sat up.

"The clouds are red!" Esclarmonde said. "They're attacking Beziers! Quickly, we must warn the elders at the school. It won't be long before Simon turns his blood-thirsty knights on Pamiers and Toulouse. And it's most certain they will attack the vulnerable first. We must warn Roger and the other lords. We don't have much time, sister! We must begin the ascent to the stronghold with the women, children, and elders."

Her beloved Occitania was divided and needed to be unified if they were to push back the northern invaders, but she belonged to the Church of the Holy Spirit and was a pacifist. How could she remain true to her spiritual beliefs as a Cathar when she needed the Occitain warriors to save them from the crusaders? It was a contradiction secretly twisting guilt in her belly. She pushed down her misgivings of violence while using every argument she could think of to convince her reluctant Occitain lords to prepare for this infamous day. Thankfully, Lord Pereille was a man of poetry and understood her prophetic admonitions from the beginning. He kept his distance from the extreme parfaits, or perfect ones, but he admired how the Cathars helped Occitania flourish. He saw how their "priests" helped the peasants harvest crops. He had watched with growing pride how Esclarmonde became the de facto leader of the Cathars over the years.

Lord Pereille admired how she helped to heal the sick and wounded, and to teach his peasants how to read. *She may be a woman*, he thought, *but she has the fire of a man! Besides, the Catholic bishops only care about filling their own bellies*! So naturally, he donated his old Visigoth and Roman stronghold on the summit at Montsegur to protect the Cathars. "The crusaders will think twice about attacking us there!" he had proclaimed to the other lords with Esclarmonde nodding in agreement at his side. He had even gone so far as to solicit the help of Templar knight, Pons Manescalci, to help them reinforce the stronghold.

"How can we trust a woman?" Pons had whispered to Lord Pereille in a meadow below the summit fortress. The Occitain lord had given Pons a reassuring nod. "She's lived with such integrity and courage, Pons," Lord Pereille begun. "She married, raised six children, and even inherited her late husband's wealth and holdings. But then, she gave it all away!"

"Gave it away?" Pons had asked, cocking his head.

"Yes, she gave it to her children, but she did it so she could dedicate her life to helping the poor and teaching the sacred Cathar wisdom to others. And her sermons...her sermons inspire everyone!"

"Interesting," Pons had said in a tone of disbelief.

"But, even before her husband died," Lord Pereille had said. "She seemed to be everywhere at once. If she wasn't building a new hospital or school, she was out helping peasants harvest their crops, build homes, or escape to the mountains when the Episcopal Inquisition threatened their lives." Pons kept silent.

Lord Pereille shrugged. "I know it's hard to believe, but it's true."

Philippa was already dressing as Esclarmonde spoke.

"We must bring the women, children, and elders to Montsegur immediately. We must move fast." Esclarmonde said, "I will warn Roger. Ride ahead and I will meet you at the school shortly."

Philippa ran out to the stables. Esclarmonde dashed up to the window and looked down to see her brother galloping away on his horse. She turned and ran down the long spiral staircase hoping to catch Roger at the front gates of the chateau. When she reached the courtyard, Esclarmonde ran into the eighteen-year-old stable boy. "Where did Roger go?"

"He is off to the Pereille Castle!" Henri replied. "He told me to tell you to bring the others to Montsegur. Simon de Montfort's armies are heading this way!"

"Yes, I know. I've seen the red skies. Did he say what shall be done with the chateau?"

"He said that Simon's armies are too large to try and fight them here. We must retreat to Montsegur where we will have a better chance of defense," Henri said.

"How big is their army?" Esclarmonde asked.

"Twenty to thirty thousand strong," Henri replied, holding his head up to summon his courage. "I must ride with you to Montsegur."

"Yes, yes, of course." Esclarmonde swallowed hard, shaking off the overwhelming size of the threat from the north. Too many times she had to steel herself like this, swallowing hard, breathing deep, holding her head high. Years of standing up to brawny knights, insolent counts and arrogant Catholic bishops who told her to sit down and be silent during theological debates. How strong she was forced to be! So strong that her tenderness was often squelched when she barked orders in the heat of the moment, hiding peasants in caves when the papal legate falsely accused them of idolatry. Sometimes, she found herself weeping in bed. That is, until a bird sang, a child hugged her, or her spirit soared in meditation.

Henri was about to run toward the stables when he saw Esclarmonde closing her eyes. He watched the great Cathar parfait enter a deep meditative state even while she stood upright. Her stature seemed to grow as her breath slowed to an imperceptible state. A soft white light emanated from the diadem on her head. Esclarmonde's scalp tingled from the warmth of the sun.

She remembered being blinded by sunlight when she was thirteen years old sitting around a banquet table outside her father's chateau in midsummer. She had listened, mesmerized as the great Cathar bishop "Papa Nicetas" told the lords, ladies, and troubadours the story of a mysterious world hidden from human eyes. She remembered standing up after the bishop's tale to announce she was ready to enter this great kingdom of light.

A troubadour sitting across from her laughed and picked up a polished shield.

"My young lady," he said, "Do you see this shield?"

Esclarmonde nodded. "Of course, I do."

The troubadour tilted the shield to reflect the sun in her eyes. Esclarmonde squinted.

"Can you see it now?" He smiled as he spoke in a pleasant voice flowing with jocularity.

"No." Esclarmonde frowned, rubbing her eyes.

The troubadour walked over to Esclarmonde and knelt before her.

"Esclarmonde, we will all shine as bright as the sun one day. But living in the light is an acquired taste, my lady. It will take thousands of surrenders in the darkness before your inner eye will open without being overwhelmed by heavenly truth."

Henri found himself entering a deep state of meditation a few feet from Esclarmonde even as the crusaders were drawing nigh. Not wanting to disturb his youthful effort, she quietly ran to the stable to fetch two horses. Trotting back to Henri with a second horse following alongside, Esclarmonde smiled as Henri opened his eyes, startled by the stomping of hooves.

"Let us ride, Henri. We must hurry to the Pereille castle."

Henri jumped on his horse and the two galloped out of the gates.

As he rode next to Esclarmonde on a back road from Chateau de Foix to the Pereille Castle, Henri glanced over to see her cape flowing with the wind around her shoulders. He marveled this great lady was almost sixty. He could barely keep up with her. No wonder the troubadours lifted her in song and praise. He must be brave like Esclarmonde. He must pray to the Holy

Spirit to know his worth.

Rounding a corner of the hidden back road to the Pereille Castle, Esclarmonde and Henri slowed their horses near the east entrance. Esclarmonde dismounted in front of the stony well and quickly tied her white steed to a post nearby.

Henri followed suit, but stopped suddenly in front of the well. Seeing Henri distraught with emotion, Esclarmonde gently walked near him. She stood silent and closed her eyes to listen to Henri's soul. She saw him remembering when he was a young boy. Soldiers threw his mother down a well and stoned her to death. The crowd cursed her blasphemy as the stones crushed her tender body. Henri was held back by a Templar Knight and heard his mother whimpering soft cries until the murmurs turned to cold silence at the bottom of a well. Esclarmonde had heard of this horrible story before, but Henri never wanted to discuss it all the years growing up in the Foix Chateau as a stable boy.

He started to weep. Esclarmonde's eyes moistened with compassion. She moved closer to him. Henri looked at her and fell into her arms crying. Esclarmonde embraced Henri with the soft warmth of her deep blue gown. "Be at peace, Henri," Esclarmonde said. "Your mother is an angel. She lives on in her true nature, just as we all will, my son. These bodies are temporary, Henri. They are corruptible. The true soul in us is eternal. We are all angels, Henri! But we must keep remembering that. Then it will be easier to be brave and do what's right."

Henri slowly stopped crying and sat on the grass. The morning sun was coming over the hills. Birds stopped singing as an ominous smoke filled the skies over Beziers where Simon de Montfort and his knights burned and slaughtered residents by order of Pope Innocent III. Henri looked up at Esclarmonde. She sat next to him. Henri smiled and plucked out a handful of grass. "Merci, Esclarmonde. I guess war and my old memories were too much for me. I haven't thought about my mother's death since you first took me into your care."

Esclarmonde held Henri's hand. "Your mother is proud of you, Henri. She sees how brave you are even if you don't feel that way at times."

Henri's eyes widened. "You can see this in me?"

"Yes. And I can see it in me too," Esclarmonde confessed. "I get scared, Henri. But I've had many more years of practicing courage than you have. If it wasn't for the teachings, our songs, prayers, confessions, meditations...if we didn't have each other to encourage each other on, even as we are doing this very moment, well Henri, I would be a complete coward!"

Henri wiped the tears from his eyes. "I see what you mean," he said. "I'm so glad we have the teachings and each other."

A quarter hour had passed when a voice rang out. "Esclarmonde! Come inside!" Roger yelled from a tower window above the castle keep. Henri stood and reached for Esclarmonde's hand. He lifted her slightly as she stood up. They both headed for the front entrance and found their way quickly to the court where a large gathering of Occitain Lords and warriors stood around a table with maps. Lord Pereille stood front and center and welcomed Esclarmonde to join in their deliberations. Roger, Esclarmonde's brother, stood at his side.

"We have very little time," Lord Pereille began. "Esclarmonde, can you gather the women, children, and elders at Dun to make the trek up to Montsegur?"

"Yes, my lord. I have already sent Philippa ahead of me to organize the caravan," Esclarmonde replied.

"Good. Your brother and those gathered here will ride out to warn the others to fortify their ramparts and accompany your caravan. How many souls do you think will be in your company?"

"I estimate about five hundred," she said.

"I'm not so sure we can convince every Lord in Pamiers to abandon their castles," Roger chimed in.

"Yes, you are right," Lord Pereille agreed. "But your Chateau de Foix may be able to resist Simon de Montfort if we work together. It is very strategic."

"A valid point," Roger said, with a swift surge of hope blazing in his eyes.

"All the lords here know the secret trails of Montsegur," Lord Pereille continued. "If Simon's knights overwhelm them on the field, they can escape with us there. It is our last hope. Montsegur is certainly the most impregnable fortress in Occitania."

"Yes, and if we defend ourselves long enough at Montsegur, we can wear them down and drain their supply lines. This will also give us time to plan our re-occupation," Lord Pereille offered.

"Excellent points," Roger agreed, searching the eyes of his fellow lords. Their heads nodded with somber approval.

"Then we are in agreement," Lord Pereille said. "Let us ride to victory for Occitania!"
"Here! Here!" The lords shouted, reaching for their swords.

Esclarmonde held her hand up. "Faith and courage, lords! Remember who you are! Remember your pretz! Hold fast to paratge!"

Roger rolled his eyes, shaking his head in embarrassment until he saw the other lords bow in a moment of silent appreciation for her words. Roger's reddened face softened to a cautious smile as he realized his sister's words were helping to encourage bravery for their cause. "Let us ride with the greatness of Occitania!" Lord Pereille commanded, shaking his sword above his head.

The nobles of Pamiers raised their swords and shouted, "Long Live Occitania!" Donning silver helmets, they followed Lord Pereille out of the chateau protected by heavy chainmail under their gleaming white tunics. Marching out to mount his horse at the west gate, Roger's eyes narrowed at his sister, Esclarmonde.

Esclarmonde returned his skeptical look with a smile. "I admire your prowess, brother. It gives our lords great courage and passion." Roger nodded. "Let us ride for Occitania!" Esclarmonde declared.

Roger turned and rode off with the other lords. Esclarmonde waved to Henri. They dashed to their horses, riding out of the east gate. But she rode not just to save innocent lives. She rode to save their sacred wisdom for the future. Esclarmonde couldn't stop thinking about their secret ancient scrolls, many of which were passed down from Gnostics, Essenes, and mysterious priestesses in ancient Egypt. How would Esclarmonde and her Cathar elders protect them now? The Inquisition would surely condemn them, toss them in the flames. And that new discovery in the walls at Montsegur. Who could she find to translate the testament of Mary Magdalene? And yet, just knowing the sacred writings existed strengthened her resolve to save her people and their wisdom.

Esclarmonde cherished her thoughts as she rode. She wondered about Papa Nicetas, his dream, their mysterious find at Montsegur. What could it all mean? As her horse carried her in undulating grace with Henri at her side, as they drew closer toward the Dun School to lead the others seeking refuge from the crusaders at the summit stronghold, as the wind pushed at their backs, speeding them forward with invisible help, she knew. Esclarmonde knew that the Holy Spirit whispered in events like these, in strange dreams and chance discoveries. She realized the divine presence was showing her that it was their responsibility to keep the writings safe. And then it came to her. She knew the perfect cave in the dark valley below Montsegur in which to hide their sacred treasures and carry the holy wisdom forward to hungry souls seeking the truth. The cave of her ancestors near Magdala Springs.

* * *

David Mampel is a former minister and semi-retired clown living in a tiny home with happy lights and coffee. He writes fiction and poetry to survive the cold, rainy darkness of Seattle and "daylights" as a full-time caregiver for his elderly parents.

THE MEANING OF DECISION

By Ayden McLane

June 30, 1916
One day before The Battle of The Somme

I stood at the window, my hands clasped behind my back, and I looked out onto the gardens, green bursting at every corner, each branch reaching toward the light. What a beautiful place, I thought, a rarity these days. I sighed. No point in standing here, doing nothing. I turned around, inspecting my surroundings. The war room was lavishly decorated, with renaissance-style murals adorning the walls. Comfortable chairs sat in a rectangle around a broad table. A crystal chandelier hung from the ceiling. Above that, dust and webs. Interesting how some people just don't look up. There was much to be seen above our heads. Sometimes a man simply needs to look up to find peace, or in my case, disturbed regret.

I send a quick prayer to God above. You never know what might help. Looking down at my hands, which were starting to wrinkle with old age, I studied my scars, heirlooms earned during active combat, trying to find the answer to that one, all-consuming question. It burned away at my mind like a disease dedicated to destroying my conscience. I closed my eyes; a knock at the door. Opening my eyes, I turned to the noise. Was it the Angel of Death, coming to exact revenge? Some demon coming to drag me down to Hell? An Archangel charging forward, his sole purpose to reprimand me?

"Come in." A plump, kindly woman peeked her head through the door, a look of concern on her face. Ella was always so worried about my health. I smiled despite myself; she was such an energetic woman, always running about, answering telegrams, taking messages, and sending letters.

"Ah, Ella. What is it?" She never bothered me while I was contemplating.

"Hello, sir. Brigadier General Winston requests an audience with you," she said this with her usual peppiness.

I sighed again, probably for the thousandth time today. Maybe it was the demon that was coming to reprimand me. "Let him in."

She nodded, then turned around and closed the door. A hundred possibilities flashed through my head. How angry would he be? Probably very. Would he threaten me? No, he wouldn't do that. Is he going to try to convince me to call off the offense? Most likely. I walked to the windowsill, waiting for the hurricane that would arrive at any moment.

I heard the door open as Ella let Winston in. I didn't turn from the window, and for a moment, there was no noise in the room, no movement, not even a breeze. Then Wilfred broke the silence.

"Ahem, General Haig, sir, I am glad that you accepted to see me." I turned. Wilfred was a stocky man with a thick neck and rough hands. Even though he looked like he could kill you, he was quite gentle. He was known to be one of the best commanders in the army. Despite all this, there were still rumors of his temper. You did not want to raise this man's ire.

"Of course." I studied him closely. He seemed calm, only slightly nervous, but I could see that was mostly a facade. Under that mask was anger. Bridled anger, but anger nonetheless.

"Sir, I implore you to change your mind on the Somme offensive. It will be a disaster, I'm sure of it." He seemed very eager, as though he had rehearsed these words a hundred times and was ready to be rid of them.

"Winston, you know how I feel about this. We are sure it will work." *I hope. What if it did fail? What if I sent all those men to die?*

"Sir, please. Those boys are going to get slaughtered."

"No, they won't. We already have them on the front lines. They will be charging in the next twenty-four hours, and I have set aside the 9th Deccan Horse regiment to push our advantage after we break through. We're just hours away from committing nine corps, nine! I cannot simply stop an attack of this scale. It is a ludicrous thought." *Please just let him listen. I don't have time to deal with this right now. I just need to think.*

"Sir, they have too many men, too many-"

I cut him off. "We have been bombing them for six and a half days straight now. We've fired over a million shells. Even more are being fired as we speak."

"They have bunkers deep in the ground! They could stay there easily for days. They'll mow down our men."

"I simply cannot believe that they can survive for that long." *They couldn't, right?*

"They can sir, they-"

I cut him off even more firmly. "Winston that is enough." I looked at him, intent on making him back down.

"But sir-" he spluttered

"No Winston."

"But *sir*-" I could see his mask cracking. He looked panicked, desperate.

"*Enough*!!" I glared at him. "Back down, General Winston," I said this with as much command as possible, letting my anger seep through.

He looked shocked, his mask completely breaking. Then, his eyes narrowed, glaring at me so intensely it made me want to take a step back. I did not. No weakness could be shown here.

"Damn you," He hissed, "Damn you! You willingly send hundreds of thousands to their deaths so that you may not seem weak by stepping down. You are weak, not wanting to admit failure. When you fail, you will seem shocked, but I know you too well. You know even now that those men are on a fool's errand, that those men are dead where they stand. But, of course, you probably know that this entire war is foolish! Already millions of lives have been wasted, and millions of more are yet to come! Those trenches, that living hell, is a death trap, a grave.

"You commit these men to the field as corpses. You talk about glory, that every capable man has a responsibility to sign up. Well, I'll tell you something, General Douglas Haig, glory is a LIE, and you DAMN WELL KNOW IT!!" He yelled that last part, spite and anger in his voice, flowing out like black tar.

It was my turn to let my mouth hang open, but I recovered quickly. "You are OUT of line General Winston!" I looked at him in anger.

"I am never out of line if my own bloody men are involved!" He shouted at me.

"You cannot demand things of me like I'm a bloody beggar!" I yelled back.

"You think you're so mighty, don't you! Like an archangel in the sky just waiting to save everyone. Do you think that this will end the war? Well, it won't! And it sure as hell won't make anything better." He roared this with a vehemence that shocked me more than anything so far. I examined him, and without his mask, he seemed a shadow of a man. A man ripped apart by fear, worry, and loss.

"Leave me," I whispered hoarsely. Winston looked at me with anger, then shuddered, tears forming at the corners of his eyes.

"I'm sorry," He paused, as though forcing himself to keep the tears at bay. "I was out of line." I looked at him incredulously. Now he feels remorse?

I grimaced. "Yes, you were." I said in that same whisper.

"I'm sorry, I just thought-" His voice cracked.

"Please, just leave me." He sighed – whether with relief or in misery, I could not tell – then walked to the door. "Please do not think poorly of me, I do what has to be done." He looked at me one last time, his features drooping, then left the room.

Ella entered, looking timid. She had heard us fighting. "Um, sir, you will need to give the order to commence the attack now, or else it will reach the soldiers too late." I looked up at her. Should I call it off? Could all of those shells have been for nothing, only disturbing enemy lines slightly? The fate of the very war might be in the balance of my decision. I had the power to end it. I was the Field Marshall, so I had the last say. I closed my eyes, hands at my temples. No, if I had a chance to end this god-forsaken war, I must take it, even if it means the lives of hundreds of thousands, if not millions.

I opened my eyes. "Send the call, they charge." Ella nodded, then scurried off to spread the message.

And with that, General Douglas Haig, Field Marshal in the British army, put his face in the palms of his hands, and wept.

* * *

Ayden McLane is a sixteen-year-old up-and-coming writer who is dedicated to teaching history in a fun and engaging way.

Rogue Wire

By Peter D. McQuade

We have it on reliable authority that those who live by the sword shall perish by the sword. We are equally aware that the pen is mightier than the sword. Yet both sword and pen pale before the power of that most wondrous and ingenious instrument of our modern age—the telegraph. And tonight, that power is putting me to a test I would rather be spared.

My name is Timothy Gladstone, but to the good folks of Silver City in the territory of Idaho, I am simply the "key tapper." Others style me the "brass pounder." By either title, I am a telegraph operator.

It is nigh on an hour since I was roused from a comfortable slumber in the warmth of my feather bed. Now I sit in frigid darkness, astride a well-mannered sorrel named Sunflower, riding the course of the wire that links Silver City to Boise City. My mission is to seek the cause of its sudden, mysterious inability to convey messages. Indeed, the line fairly overflows with a torrent of mad, undecipherable electrical impulses.

I fear this will be nothing as mundane or easily remedied as a line break, or a cracked insulator, or improperly filled battery jars. In the dozen years of my career—which began in the War as a greenhorn telegrapher with the Army of the Potomac—I've never witnessed anything so bizarre as this sudden aberration. Furthermore, the safety and security of tomorrow's outgoing silver shipment teeters in the balance. For, although the wagons will be escorted by the usual retinue of armed guards, only the telegraph can provide the sheriffs of the two counties along the route with timely notice as to the shipment's departure. And only the telegraph is able to track its progress through the towns along the way. Thus, the line must be fixed, and I have no recourse but to answer this call to duty.

I am grateful for the company of a quick-witted Nez Perce messenger boy of sixteen who rides a sturdy, Dalmatian-spotted Appaloosa. My companion's English name is Darius. His horse's name I cannot spell and am but poorly able to pronounce. I am pleased that Darius aspires to the key tapper's vocation. Already, his fingers are able to tap out the Morse code with the swift certainty of a mountain goat scaling the granite spires and ramparts of the nearby mountains.

The undulating wagon road before us roils with ghostly shadows cast by the miner's kerosene lantern clutched in my left hand. A bone-numbing December wind howls like a pack of wolves hailing the light of a full moon. But this night there is no moon. The sky is a black velvet carpet upon which a cache of diamonds has been strewn. The planet Mars glows red like a railroad switch lamp—or one of those red lamps of a different purpose I have witnessed, from a prudent distance of course, in second-floor windows on the backstreets of my hometown in New Jersey.

Darius calls to me, his voice raised against the wind. "The silver shipment to Boise City must be mightily urgent. Else why would the Black Jack Mill not wait to dispatch a lineman to do the job tomorrow, in daylight?" The lantern light sets Darius's dark, Nez Perce eyes to glimmering.

I shrug to fend off the chill. "Our orders are to ensure the line is working by noontime."

"Timothy, you are a telegraph operator, not a lineman."

"Duty calls," I reply. "Tonight, I will be a lineman."

Darius lifts his gaze to the stars. "The moon sleeps. Perhaps another time would be better."

Indeed, I muse, *how welcome a bit of moonlight would be.*

"I've been through worse," I mumble. My mind casts an inward glance to a time a decade ago and a place two thousand miles distant—a swamp on the periphery of Richmond, Virginia.

* * *

I am clinging to the branches of a bendy oak. Shrieking hornet-swarms of Rebel bullets shred the leaves around me. I am but sixteen years of age and am stringing a line at General Weitzel's orders. Upon a wilderness floor drenched in scarlet, a dozen men moan prayers and epithets with their final breaths. I continue my work, for a glorious victory for our Union Forces hangs by this thin wire.

From behind a row of bushes, a rifle barrel glints in the sun. "There he is!" a Southern voice shouts. Another joins in, "It's the Yankee brass pounder!"

The rifle muzzle slews toward my direction. "Kill the bastard!" one of the voices bellows.

* * *

I shake my head to cast away the memory, murmuring a prayer of thanksgiving that the Rebel gunman had missed, before he himself was felled by a Union bullet.

"Yes, I've been through worse," I say again to Darius.

We move on, up the side of one hill and down the next, passing one telegraph pole then another, always straining to glimpse the occasional sparkle of lantern light on copper wire. This line connects Silver City to Boise City—and to the world. By this means has mankind harnessed the lightning bolts of Zeus for the noble purpose of rapid communion among the peoples of the Earth. And sadly, as I learned in the War, for far less peaceful endeavors. The wire is barely six months old, and until this night, it has been beset by remarkably few troubles. So far as Darius and I have been able to discern, the cable is in fine fettle—save for having gone mad.

Somewhere over the near ridgeline, a coyote lets out a blood-chilling screech that metamorphoses into a prolonged, wavering banshee howl. In a moment, it is joined by a ghoulish chorus of coyotes.

With one hand, I haul back on the reins and Sunflower slows, then halts. She whinnies and swings her head, side to side. She would rather launch into a full gallop, plunging into the black abyss, anywhere to flee the diabolical choir. I briefly let go the reins and feel for the hand grip of the Colt revolver in my holster. Its touch is reassuring.

I look to Darius. His unperturbed eyes convey a conviction that Coyote, true friend to humankind, is simply being playful tonight. Yet he doesn't smile. "Humans," he says, "they are the true menace. Nature is animated by neither greed nor deception."

Underneath my legs, Sunflower snorts and strains against the reins.

"If we aren't looking for a break in the line," Darius says, "then what do you expect to find?"

"The line's not dead," I reply. "If anything, it's too much alive."

"With gibberish. You said that earlier." He jabs a finger toward the strand of copper above us. My eyes narrow. "Yes, gibberish. Like nothing I've ever heard."

We continue on the road, our horses progressing gingerly, skittishly.

"It's a long way to Boise City," Darius replies. "And the wind is angry."

I attempt to reassure him. "No doubt, other linemen will have left Boise by now, searching in our direction. At worst, we'll meet them halfway, in daylight."

Suddenly Sunflower lurches to the left and thrusts her head sideways. Her eyes are wide with terror. She tries to run, but I check her, my knees jammed tightly against the saddle. Her hooves scar the frozen ground and she jerks to a halt at the roadside. She protests with a mournful, gargled grunt.

"What's the matter, girl?" I call, as soothingly as I can. The swaying lantern sends devil shadows dancing through the sagebrush.

Suddenly a dark specter races wildly across the road, averting a collision with Darius's horse by mere inches. Then it is gone.

"Antelope," Darius says, shaking his head. "Spooked.... Sunflower heard it coming."

I swing the lantern around and find no other creatures in proximity. I rub my horse's neck and murmur gentle things to her. Then, slowly, haltingly, we continue.

"Antelope don't spook without reason," Darius says. "Something is amiss—something beyond our ken."

The road dips and we pass through shallow snowdrifts. Instinctively, I sense that, in the wire high above us, the rogue electrical pulses continue insanely to surge and rattle. No dots and dashes, no intelligent message. Not the bolts of Zeus, harnessed and benign, but rather the malevolent darts and curses of his daughter Eris, the goddess of chaos. I think it again, *The line is beyond inoperative. It has gone mad.*

Without warning, the blackness overhead lightens to slate gray. "How could that be?" I murmur. "There's no moon, and dawn is hours away." Beneath the woolen collar of my coat, the skin crawls on the back of my neck.

Cresting a ridgeline, we pull up next to another telegraph pole. My mouth hangs open, as does Darius's. Far to the north, the sky above the mountains writhes and swells in streaky waves of phosphorescent green. Could it be the depths of hell have opened before us? I hear the echoes of Darius's warning—*Perhaps another time would be better.*

"Heaven help us," Darius finally mumbles, his face distorted by the ghastly glow of the phantasmagoria.

"Has the Aurora ever come this far south before?" I ask.

"I've never seen it."

"One could read by this light," I say, with but little exaggeration.

"It is a sign," he says. "The heavens themselves are angry. Even the animals are fearful. We must go back."

I am inclined to agree. However, the call of duty gnaws at the very foundation of my soul. I dismount.

"What are you doing?" Darius asks.

"I'm going to tap the line."

His expression says, *Have you lost your mind?*

"With this light, it'll be much easier than in the dark." I hand Darius the lantern, whose light is feeble in comparison with the Aurora. I open my saddlebag and fish out a wire-cutter, a hammer, a pouch of large nails and a coil of wire. I cut a several-yards length of wire and stash it in my coat pocket.

Darius watches in tight-jawed silence.

"This won't take but a few minutes," I say. "I was one of the best wire-tappers in the Army. At times, I knew as much about Rebel war plans as did their generals in the field."

"Nevertheless," Darius says, "we should come back in daylight."

I am already pounding a nail into the pole. A moment later, I hoist myself onto it. By the light of the gyrating green sky, I pound a second nail. As I work, my thoughts turn to tomorrow's silver shipment to Boise City. This telegraph line is essential to its safety.

Soon I am hugging the top of the pole. Below me, Darius's shadow dances to the silent auroral rhythm. Over my right shoulder, in a distant valley invisible from here, Silver City sleeps peacefully.

I remove my right glove and drop it to the ground. I grasp the cutter.

Wire-tapping is a simple matter, I remind myself as my heart races. *With proper care, there is no danger, as the electrical voltage is too small to cause harm.*

The coyotes now howl without pause, answering the call of the strange green heavens. Sunflower whinnies.

"You're fighting Nature," Darius calls. "Don't do it."

I shake my head.

He continues, "Whatever it is that brought the Northern Lights here is also what has possessed the wire."

I must admit this possibility makes a modicum of sense, but I give no reply.

"Don't challenge the spirits of the night realm," he pleads.

"You're being superstitious," I shout over the wind. With one arm, I embrace the pole. With the other, I lean and stretch toward the wire.

"No, Timothy!" he shouts.

"You said it before—Nature isn't the danger. There's no greed or deception in it."

"Listen to me!" Darius implores. "The Sun is restless, the Darkness is in distress. Ghosts will be on the prowl."

"Don't bother me now." I steady my boot's heel between the pole and the top-most nail. My right arm strains as trembling fingertips reach for the wire. Darius's mouth gapes in anticipation.

Suddenly the wire snaps. A shower of orange sparks blinds me. Goddess Eris has flung a thousand darts into my flesh, and every nerve in my body rings with the gibberish of the rogue wire. The world around me becomes hazy and I am filled with a sensation of being drawn into the thin copper strand.

* * *

How much time has passed? Seconds? Minutes? Perhaps hours? I struggle to force my eyelids open. The devilish green Aurora is gone. I am in daylight. I am clinging to the upper branches of a young oak tree. Darius and the horses are nowhere to be seen.

Gradually, I realize I am no longer in the mountains of Idaho, but rather in a Virginia swamp. The breeze is pungent with smoke and death. Richmond is burning.

Below me, a few paces distant, a blue-jacketed soldier gasps his dying breath. A voice shouts to me, "Hurry, boy, hurry! We need that line now!" It is General Weitzel.

Clutching an uncoiling length of telegraph wire in my right hand, I reach to fasten it to a branch.

A rustling in the bushes thirty yards away commands my attention. From out of the cover, a rifle barrel glints in the sun. "There he is!" a voice shouts. It is a Southern voice.

Another joins in, "It's the Yankee brass pounder."

My hand tightens around the wire. Through bare fingers, without even the aid of a telegraph key, I feel the gibberish within it.

The rifle muzzle slews toward my direction. "Kill the bastard!" one of the voices bellows.

The gun belches yellow flame and white smoke.

Before the sound of the blast reaches my ears, the impact has already rammed into my left shoulder. I fall through space, still clutching the wire.

* * *

I am in a strange bed in a strange room. Unfamiliar voices mutter. I draw in a raspy, labored breath. The warm air is heavy with the smell of ether. My body is wracked with pain, from crown to sole, and my immediate impulse is to return to the nothingness of slumber.

However, a softly-spoken entreaty halts my retreat. "Can you hear me?" Unlike the others, this voice is familiar. I blink several times, until I am able to associate the person's slowly emerging image with his voice. It is Darius. He is standing a few paces away, his hat in his hand.

"Where am I?" I croak.

"In the infirmary," he says. "In Silver City."

"Not Richmond?" I reply.

Darius seems quizzical. "Richmond? No."

Gentle hands lift my head and press a water glass to my lips. I sip.

"What day is this?" I ask.

"Monday." Darius steps closer. "You have been unconscious for two days and three nights."

My left leg is afire, and my chest feels as if it has been trampled by a wild horse. "Did the silver shipment make it to Boise City?" I ask.

"Yes," Darius says.

"Good," I reply, struggling to roll to my side. I am unable to do so, for my torso is tightly bandaged and my leg is splinted.

"Your leg was broken in your fall from the pole," Darius says. "The doctor assures us it will heal in a month."

"You saved me," I murmur. "Thank you."

Darius smiles. "There's something you'll be pleased to know," he says.

"What?" I ask, signaling the nurse I need more water.

"The telegraph line is working as if nothing had ever happened."

My eyes become wide as an owl's at midnight. "What about the gibberish?"

"It's gone," Darius says, laying a hand on mine. "Not a shred is left."

"Gone?" I moan.

"Yes, and there is an explanation for it."

I nod for him to go on.

"Telegraph operators from many nations experienced difficulties that night. There is much chatting about it on the wire today." He pauses for me to comprehend.

"And?" I ask.

"An astronomer in England swears it was the result of a disturbance of the Sun—some kind of storm on its surface."

My nose wrinkles and I groan. "A storm on the Sun? Hogwash!"

"They say it's happened before," Darius says, "seventeen years ago. It wreaked havoc with telegraphs—operators suffered electrical shocks."

I shut my eyes against the pain.

"In addition," Darius continues, "it caused an impressive southward migration of the Aurora Borealis."

The twin images of orange sparks and the hellish green-and-black sky threaten to overwhelm me. I blurt, "How could there be a storm on the sun? It has no clouds."

"How am I to know?" Darius replies, shrugging. "I'm just a key tapper, not a scientist."

The nurse offers me more water. Its coolness is calming. "Nevertheless," I say, "the English astronomer's assertion is...intriguing. As even hogwash can be."

Darius's grin brings me a glimmer of comfort.

"If what he and you say is true," I continue, "then there was a natural cause for all we endured that night." I sigh at the thought and relax a bit more. "And Richmond...was nothing more than a very bad dream."

"Regardless," Darius interjects, "tapping the wire was unwise."

I sneer. "What are you getting at?"

"You challenged the spirits of the night realm."

I sense my face is flushing. "That's superstitious nonsense!"

My companion continues, his eyes now brimming with unwelcomed pity. "We were alone on the hill that night, you and I. And I couldn't have done it—you can trust my word. It had to be the spirits...."

"You're making no sense," I say.

Darius fidgets with his hat. "It was the spirits, all right." His voice is calm and reverent. "I find no other logical way to explain it."

"Explain what, for God's sake?"

Darius points to my left shoulder. "Your bullet wound."

* * *

Peter D. McQuade grew up wandering the mountains and deserts of Idaho. When he was six, his parents made the mistake of letting him stay up late to watch *Wagon Train*, *Bonanza*, and *The Twilight Zone*. Pete now resides in Colorado and when he's not writing fiction, he's a professor of Space Systems Engineering—sort of a wagonwright on the cosmic frontier. His short stories have been published in *Bewildering Stories*, *Adelaide Literary Magazine*, and the *2022 Pikes Peak Writers Anthology*. Follow him at PeteMcQuade.com.

Tintinnabulation

By Sue Petty

CLANG. CLANG. CLANG.

The sun sulks through the window, casting a dull light over two slight mounds under a heavy patchwork quilt. Annie pokes her nose out of the warm sanctuary, anticipating the nip of morning air. She sheds the quilt with a quick flick of her arm and pulls on her clothes: the coarse cloth grates her young skin, and her knees momentarily buckle under the weight of her work apron. She tames her long fair hair into a neat tight bun, accomplished without the aid of her right little finger, which the loom had robbed a month earlier. Grabbing her white mob cap off the end of the bed, she tiptoes across the floorboards, careful not to wake her younger sister, Jessie, who, age six, has four more years till she will adopt the same routine.

In the scullery, her mother saws thick slices of bread for breakfast. Bent-backed and red-cheeked, she flashes her daughter a smile. 'Come on, Annie, love. Tea's brewing.'

Annie rubs her bare arms, and the goosebumps recede in the heat emanating from the roaring fire. She looks round for her father. There he is, slouched in his armchair by the fender, gnawing on a crust. The fiery flames give him a crimson glow, and the sweat seeps from the crags in his face like soulful tears. She tries to catch his eye, but he looks away with a bewildered expression that resembles a tormented demon tired of the toils of this world and homesick for his own hell. He sighs and scratches his whiskers, trying to solve a riddle long forgotten. His absences from the mill are becoming regular. Annie grits her teeth and purses her lips. She resents his selfish moodiness and emotional detachment and longs to kick him into action. 'Get off your lazy arse,' she wants to yell.

'He'll be all right, love. He just needs a rest.' Her mother puts his apathy down to an unexplained illness.

Is it contagious? Annie wonders, because the man next door suffers a similar ailment. Her father wheezes and coughs-up a globule of green phlegm. He spits into the fire and it ignites into a cloud of toxic fumes, then sizzles into nothing.

A week old baby gurgles from a makeshift cot in the corner, and another child toddles across the floor babbling incoherently, the world still new and appealing. The threadbare rug falls two feet short of the wall, and a splinter in the exposed floorboards impales the child's tender sole. Mam sweeps him up in loving arms, and dangles a picture of baby Jesus, Mary, and Joseph the vicar had given out at church, to stop the crying. She has subjected all her children to colourful images and captivating stories from the Bible: stories of suffering, hope, and salvation. They learnt to read by reading extracts from scripture out loud to the family, every Sunday evening.

Annie gulps down the tea, scalding her throat but warming her insides. 'I'll be late home, Mam. Promised Sarah I'd go to some meeting after work.'

The door slams on her way out.

* * *

Twelve hours since Annie had left the house. She stretches her aching back and soothes her sore fingers with her tongue. Putting on her coat, she glances out the factory window. Weary workers stumble through the tall iron gates like over-milked cattle, heads bent, bracing against the evening chill. A young woman looks around, stoops to pick up a shilling glistening in the mud and slips it in her pocket, not believing her luck. In the distance, rows of terraced houses beckon with unfulfilled promises of homely satisfaction. Between the scorched chimney pots a pale full moon ascends the twilight sky, a bright star close behind, winking in the lunar aura.

Annie had noticed the posters dotted around the canteen, during dinner break, but Votes for Women means nothing to her. She wants to go home and put her feet up, but Sarah tugs at her sleeve.

'Aw, come on Annie. You promised. Besides, it'll be fun.'

Annie gives in and, linking arms, they head for the canteen.

* * *

A dozen factory girls turn-up for the meeting: some out of curiosity; some to postpone going home; and a few, like Sarah, who want to know more about the Women's Suffrage Movement. They stand in tired little groups, gossiping about the day's occurrences. Gladys is in the family way, again. Ethel's on the streets, can't pay the rent. The manager has sacked Mary, no one knows why. All the usual.

It goes quiet and Annie looks towards the door. She recognises the woman from the posters in the canteen: round handsome face, dark-brown hair done up in a tight-bun - a few stragglers make a charming contrast with her pale complexion. She wears a long brown skirt and a white silk blouse with a high collar. A sash of three horizontal stripes: green, white and purple runs across her breast, from right shoulder to left hip. A brown, flat-topped peaked bonnet tops off the outfit, reminding Annie of an army Captain she had seen in the penny newspaper.

Another woman follows closely behind, similarly attired. But older and taller, straight-backed with a Sergeant Major demeanour and a no-nonsense expression. She carries a leather attaché case and a pile of leaflets. She takes a rear seat, while the other woman remains standing.

The woman smiles even white teeth and addresses her audience in a low, well-bred voice. 'Good evening, ladies. Thank you so much for coming.'

Her presence fills the room. Her voice fluctuates like the ebb and flow of life itself, and Annie clings to it like a drowning creature. The woman's eyes change colour chameleon-like, matching every phrase and passionate resolve: purple for loyalty, white for purity and green for hope. They grow misty, then flash like beacons on a foggy night, drawing Annie in like a lost soul at sea.

Enthralled, Annie doesn't understand what the woman is talking about at first, then several words strike home.

'Long hours... low pay... women's rights.'

Annie listens with more intent. Her cheeks flush, her heart races and her eyes turn misty too. She takes a deep breath and nudges her friend.

'Sarah, she's talking about us!'

At the end of the meeting, the woman makes a plea for the factory workers to join the Women's Cause, to become trade union members, and to spread the word amongst their fellow workers. The Sergeant Major steps forward and produces a pencil and paper to jot down names on a roll call of political consciousness.

Grasping her friend's arm, Annie leads her forward.

'Come on, Sarah. Let's do it.' She is shy and out of her depth, but this is bigger than herself. She must be a part of it.

* * *

That night, the woman's words reverberate through Annie's mind, and she lies awake, thinking of all the best things she said. Things about what women can achieve if they stick together; if they can have a say in politics. Things *can* change.

The sunlight sears through the rags at the window, illuminating two slight mounds under a heavy quilt. The clang of the factory bell rouses Annie from her dreams, and she jumps out of bed oblivious to the cold air nipping her skin. A fire is igniting in her heart and soul. There is work to do, but a different work. It is another morning, but a bright new day.

* * *

Sue Petty is a writer from Leicestershire in the UK. She is currently working on a collection of short stories entitled *Women of the Working Class.*

THE GODS OF GREEN COUNTY

By Mary Elizabeth Pope

My brother Buddy's blood stained the pavement of Main Street for weeks after he was murdered. In the drought of 1926, nobody in Arkansas would use what water they did have to clean up a sidewalk, so I passed that spot on my way to the Church of Divine Holiness to worship, or Merle's Grocery to pick up cornmeal, or Harvey's Hardware to buy a hinge I needed for Mama's cupboard since Buddy wasn't around to fix it anymore. That stain turned from bright red to dark brown, then faded to a dirty gray, until the edges began to flake away in the hot July breeze. I could've walked another way, I know. I could've turned down Oak Street or Linden Lane and cut over. But I just couldn't stop walking past that spot every chance I got, and I was really sorry when it finally washed away in the rainstorm all the farmers had been praying for because I was sure it was the last of my brother I'd ever see.

Turns out I was wrong. A month later I woke up to a moon so full I thought it was morning, and when I lifted the curtain, I could see Buddy in the yard looking up at me.

"Buddy?" I called out. "Buddy? Oh, Buddy. It's really you." But the next thing I knew, my sister Shelby was on top of me, shaking me to keep quiet or I'd wake Mama.

"Buddy's out there," I said.

"Sure he is. Along with Daddy, I know," Shelby said. "Now quit talking nonsense and go back to sleep. You're just seeing things again, that's all." So I laid down and waited, but by the time her breathing evened out and I pushed back the curtain, Buddy was gone.

Truth is, I always could see things. Not every little thing all the time, but the full flower inside the bud of a rose, the fire inside a new green leaf that wouldn't show until fall, the old man inside the boy selling newspapers on the street. Sometimes I even knew the future. One summer when a hard frost killed the crops and everybody was hungry, I had a vision of Johnny Wilcox bringing us a wheelbarrow full of turnips, and sure enough, he showed up the next day. Another time, I saw Laverne Bishop take up a snake even though she'd never tested her faith before, and the very next Sunday she did. Those times, Mama called me her little prophet. Most of the time she said it was Satan working through me.

Maybe my visions were the reason she was so much harder on me than she was on Shelby. "Those are the neatest stitches I've ever seen," Mama would say when Shelby hemmed a tablecloth. Or if she put on a dress, Mama would say, "My word, Shelby, that gingham is so flattering on you." So I'd work real hard on my sewing and press my calico extra good hoping Mama might notice me too, but all Mama ever noticed were the places I'd missed when I wiped the supper table, or which dishes weren't dry when I'd put them in the cupboard, or that my hair was so curly it looked like a rat's nest.

She rarely had a kind word for my brother Buddy neither, no matter how many catfish he caught or rabbits he shot or how nice he'd fixed the post on the front porch, but for some reason Buddy didn't take it personal. Maybe it's because he always found ways to get Mama back: he'd hide a handful of toads in Mama's bed, or fill her sugar bowl with salt, or stroll through the living room in his drawers when Mama was holding a church meeting. I suppose I could've tried getting back at her too, but it wasn't in me. Still, whenever I'd get to feeling real low, Buddy would come sit beside me on the back porch where I'd go to hide my tears.

After a while he'd say, "Coralee, just because Mama can't see you're special don't mean it's not true."

"I know," I'd say. And for a while I would know, until the next time Mama was mean.

So when Buddy came home one day and told us he was heading to the Ozarks for a job laying tracks for a new railway, I knew I couldn't stay. I would've never left otherwise. It was the start of the cotton harvest, and I loved waking up in the mornings before sunrise and heading out into the fields before it got hot while most folks were still asleep. I loved smelling the good earth, wet with dew, and seeing the light spread across the big sky. I loved how something so light as cotton got heavier the more I put into my sack, and how, when I dragged it to the scale, Mr. Jenks always said, "Miss Coralee, I do believe that is your biggest haul yet."

Buddy had been gone a week when my cousin Darlene came home for a visit from Michigan and told me about her job waiting tables at Myrtle's Hotel in Flint, making twice the pay I made in the fields. She told me I could work there too, even board for free. When I told Mama I was going, she didn't try to stop me. I hoped she might, right up until the day Darlene's daddy drove us to the station in Memphis. I was wearing my nicest dress and hat, and I'd already said goodbye to Mama and Shelby. I was about to step into the truck when Mama ran off the porch and hugged me so tight it near knocked the wind out of me. She said, "You look so pretty, Coralee, all ready for the big city." And I thought, *Oh, Mama, why now?* That was just like Mama, to push me to the point of giving up, only to reel me back in at just the moment it was too late to turn back.

When I came home a year later, I hoped maybe Mama had missed me, even if she never did return the telegram I sent her saying I was married. But when I walked in the house with my bags, she didn't even ask what I was doing there. She just said, "Shelby, put on another plate for supper."

See, Mama always said the only man a woman could truly rely on was the Lord. My own daddy drank himself to death, and before that Mama had a husband named Elbert who ran off after only a year. Maybe that's why she turned to the Lord. Maybe that's why she taught me that to love any man before Him was false. Which I had fully believed until the night Chess Collins walked into Myrtle's Hotel a month after I moved up to Flint. That's when I learned it was a lot harder to love the Lord more than a man, especially when that particular man was seated at one of your tables, saying it just wasn't possible for a girl to look so fresh after the long shift I'd worked, and had I heard about the dances at Flint Park, and might I cut a rug with him one night?

Chess had the gift for talk I'd never had, but he seemed happy enough just to have me listen. But even though Chess and me was married in church, it didn't take long to know Chess was not a man of God. Not even a man of his own word. He'd promised to give up drinking, but I could smell the gin on his breath not two weeks after we'd said our vows. I pled with him for months. I begged him to stop. Then one morning before Chess came to from some bender he'd been on, I did something I do not know how I ever found the strength to do. Must've been the Holy Spirit made me pack my bags. Must've been the Holy Spirit made me put on my coat. Because if it was only me deciding, I would've never left Chess. I could not imagine never waking up beside him again, never seeing his eyes crinkle when he smiled, never hearing him say, "Why don't you come on over here and give old Chess some sugar?"

The shame I felt living in Mama's house after a failed marriage was bad enough, but the shame I felt living back in Paradise was worse. Customers at the Dew Drop Inn looked away when I smiled, or seemed not to recognize me buying gloves at Miss Jane's Finery. Only place anyone met my eyes was the Church of Divine Holiness, where Brother Jeremiah Cassidy said the good Lord would forgive me. But folks in Paradise did not seem like they would ever forget. Only person who ever made me feel any better about my time with Chess was Buddy, who'd come back from the Ozarks only a few weeks before I got home.

"So what? You married him," Buddy said one night when I shared my shame with him on the back porch. It was the coolest place you could sit, which is where you could find us most nights.

"You loved him?" And I said I did love Chess, but now I felt foolish about the whole mess, like I should've known from the get-go that he was trouble.

"How can you know a thing like that? Oh, that's right, tell the future, can't you?" Buddy teased.

"Sometimes," I said. Buddy always got a bang out of the things I could see.

But he just said, "You loved that man, Coralee. Ain't no shame in that. Trying not to love somebody you feel for, who feels for you, well, that'd be the real shame." Buddy's ideas about love made sense somehow, even if they didn't quite match up with what I knew of the Lord's, and what he said made me feel better whenever I thought of it that way.

But one day, helping Mama cook supper, she said, "I wouldn't put much stock in what Buddy says if I was you."

"You been listening to us, Mama?"

"You think I can't hear you crying Buddy a river over Chess Collins every night?"

"Buddy's just trying to help."

"That boy's full of the devil, Coralee."

"He's all right, Mama," I said. "He's just the same."

"People change, Coralee. You got a lot of learning left to do, and one divorce under your belt already." The papers had come in the mail just the week before, with Chess's signature on them. He had not even tried to get me back.

That night after supper, as I sat out in the cool evening air with Buddy, I said, "Why's Mama mad at you?"

Buddy didn't say anything right away, and he didn't look at me neither. Finally he said, "What happened between me and Mama is between me and Mama. You best keep out of it."

"Still," I started to say, but Buddy cut me off.

"Mama's got a right to be mad if she wants to be," he said.

Now I didn't know what Buddy meant by this, but I didn't press the matter further, partly because without me really noticing it, we'd somehow begun to see less of Buddy and I was afraid if I brought up Mama again, I'd lose even those few nights I still got to spend with him. Mama was no company at all, and Shelby wasn't one for chitchat. All she'd said when I came home from Flint was, "There's more fish in the sea than ever came out of it." And for her it was that simple. She didn't have that way of feeling someone else's pain that Buddy had in him.

Sometimes Buddy'd turn up before supper and give Mama a duck he'd shot or a string of crappie he'd caught. After a while, though, he'd be out all night and I'd wake up and see his bed still made, and I began to wonder if what Mama said about him changing was true after all.

Then a few months on, for a string of nights, Buddy was home again. He sat longer than usual out in the cool backyard with me, talking late into the evening. I had no idea where he'd been and no idea why he'd come home, but night after night, he seemed better than ever—no pranks, no fooling, just all grown up. And right before we went off to bed one night, he gave me one of his playful hugs and said, "You're a good girl, Coralee. I want to see you smile again. You got to let go of Chess Collins and move on with your life. Be happy." And looking across the hall that night, seeing Buddy safe in his bed just as I tucked myself into mine, I thanked the Lord and went to sleep with a smile on my lips.

But early the next morning came a knock on the front door, and for some reason I looked across at Buddy's room and could see his bed already made. Which was strange, since Buddy never made his bed. Mama always said that if cleanliness was next to godliness, Buddy was going straight to hell.

Well, I ran down the stairs to answer the door but Mama beat me to it, and there stood Buddy's friend Luther Jackson on the little porch. He held his hat in his hand, respectful-like, but he looked terrible. He stared at the floor for a long moment and finally said, "I'm so sorry to be the one to tell y'all, but Buddy was shot dead this morning."

Mama put her hand up to the doorframe, opened her mouth to speak, then fainted straightaway. I thought I'd be next, the way my knees were shaking, so I sank down on the steps and leaned my head against the wall.

"Who done it?" Shelby asked. She'd broken Mama's fall and was cradling her head.

"The Green County sheriff, Wiley Slocum. That's all I know. Some scuffle next to the tavern. Y'all need get down to the courthouse in Stillwater now."

Later, we heard Sheriff Slocum caught Buddy climbing out a window of the Paradise Tavern with a pocketful of cash he'd stolen, and when Buddy picked up a crowbar to defend himself, the sheriff had shot him. But my brother Buddy was no thief. And I knew that boy would not hurt a fly. So I looked forward to that hearing because I knew the law would clear things right up. But when the verdict came back that there was not enough evidence to charge Sheriff Slocum for killing Buddy in anything but self-defense, I could only watch that man let out a sigh of relief. I could only wonder how I'd ever learn to live with the sin of my despair.

Luckily, Mr. Jenks had taken me back on his crew, and even if my job at Myrtle's Hotel had been high-class, I was happy to head out to the fields before sunup to start picking cotton again. I'd get so focused on making weight that I could all but forget that Buddy was dead and the law was a sham, or that I ever knew Chess Collins, let alone married him. Maybe that's why I worked so hard. Maybe that's why I took extra shifts until Mama said I'd ruin my health. But only work could keep those terrible thoughts away.

Then a few years on, Earl Wilkins asked me to dance at a social down to the gazebo. Shelby talked me into going. She was married by then with two kids and just dying for some grown-up talk, and maybe I was ready to move on in some way I didn't know yet, because even though I didn't want to go, I went with her.

Now, I'd known Earl all my life. Thought him a fine fellow, as everyone did. He wasn't flashy like Chess. He wasn't trying to charm or flatter me. He just brought me a Coca-Cola. Told me about his job at the cotton gin in Boone. Asked me what it was like to live in a city big as Flint. He was handsome in a way I'd never noticed, maybe because he hadn't noticed it himself, didn't wear his good looks like Chess did, polished up to a shine. Earl didn't need no shine: he was tall and broad-shouldered and square-jawed, and I liked his quiet way, the seriousness in his eyes when he looked at me. And the day Earl asked me to marry him, I felt happy in a way I didn't know I could again after believing Chess had ruined me for good and all. Earl even agreed to a church wedding, though he was not a church-going man, I'm sorry to say. But he cared about it because it was what I wanted. That was just how Earl was.

Still, there was one thing I had to ask Mama before I left home. I knew I'd never have the chance again. So the night before the wedding, I worked up the nerve to say, "Mama, why were you so mad at Buddy when he died?"

"Don't ask me to speak ill of the dead, Coralee."

"I'm not, Mama. I just want to know what happened is all."

"No, Coralee, you don't," Mama said. "You never would hear a word against that boy, and now it's too late." And I cried myself to sleep that night, knowing then that Mama would never tell.

But in the morning, Earl was waiting at Church of Divine Holiness with a smile on his face. I could still feel the hurt about Mama as we took our vows before Brother Jeremiah, but they say God never closes a door without opening a window. And as we drove past Mama's house on the way to start our new life together, I knew Earl was the window God opened for me.

* * *

Mary Elizabeth Pope is the author of a collection of short fiction, *Divining Venus Stories* (The Waywiser Press, 2013), and the historical novel *The Gods of Green County* (Blair, 2021). Her stories and essays have also appeared in such literary magazines as *Florida Review*, *Arkansas Review*, *Bellingham Review*, *Passages North*, *Ascent*, *Fugue*, and many others. She holds a Ph.D. in English and Creative Writing from University of Iowa, and is Professor of English at Emmanuel College in Boston.

This is an excerpt from her novel *The Gods of Green County* (Blair).

Cinnabar for the Funeral

By Jennie Treverton

On the morning of her husband's funeral Lollia Saepia sat in voluminous black in the armchair at her bedroom's east window, the one with the view of the new aqueduct lately sliced through town all the way from the eastern hills. While the slave Felica worked behind her, carrying the curling-iron to and from the brazier, Lollia held up the heavy bronze mirror that had been part of her dowry twelve years ago. She saw that Felica had well understood the instruction. A loose wave with ringlets teased apart to give the wild effect. Apart from her husband and one or two of the slaves, nobody had seen Lollia's hair uncurled since the funeral of her father when she was a child of six. Nobody knew how flat and lifeless it was. Today of all days, nobody would find out.

She held out the mirror for Felica to take and said, 'The darker rouge. Give it to me.'

The tiny jar had been a gift from her husband, given via his body-servant. The one thing she remembered about that slave, dead now to malaria: his receding hairline when he made his bow, how neatly symmetrical, nearly architectural: *On the birth of your daughter. With deep affection.*

The slave placed the mirror with care on the table, picked up the jar and turned back to the mistress. As Lollia took it, momentarily their eyes met. Felica showed the proper shame and lowered her gaze, but too late, for Lollia had read it. *Rouge, today?* But she felt no anger. The girl couldn't be expected to understand. She held it up to the window. The jar was half-empty, its inside dirty with finger-scoops so that the light shone dim through the coloured glass. A disappointing effect. Nearby a single bird chirruped over the powerful gush of the courtyard fountain which thanks to the aqueduct drowned out much of the street noise. Not like when she first came to live in her husband's house: so many difficult nights. All gone now.

'Come closer, Felica.'

The slave hesitated. Lollia let the moment hang. Let the child feel some fear. One by one Lollia dipped each finger in, scraping her nails across the soft surface.

'Closer. Bring your face to me.'

When her clawed nails touched Felica's cheek the girl's eyes squeezed shut, but she didn't flinch or move away. Lollia applied just enough pressure to look like grief, but while the rouge made convincing weals, it was too brown.

'Fetch the other. The cinnabar.'

With deep affection. In Hades Marcus was watching, purple-faced. Artifice, lies: his uprightness: she felt it. And yet she would not scar her cheeks, much less jump on the pyre as her children watched. Enough had been spent on gilt-horned sacrifices from what he'd left. She took the cinnabar, held it up: yes. With care she loaded the nails of both hands with only a scrape under each. At the right moment—when? When the body caught a light?—when she felt the congregation to be ready, their expectation cresting, then would she step forward and announce her grief with a wail, fall to her knees, lift her bloodied face.Yes. Not only he watched from the Underworld but also her parents, her mother, reminding her not to tear her hair but leave her beautiful curls alone, and above all else stay out of the rain, for no wealthy suitors would love an untidy maiden with rain-flattened hair. Among Marcus's many friends there were magistrates and aristocrats with names even older than his. This house, the villas, the slaves, the children. Everything.

Waiting for instruction, Felica stood with dirtied cheeks, looking upset. Silly child. Lollia pretended not to notice. She exhaled, looked out and saw, over the hills, the white sky blurring to grey.

The sight made her want to cry, a swelling pain like she'd felt yesterday in his dark study with the lawyer and the scribe with the account books. Listening to them speak she had managed to hold the tears back: now let them come, let them run but dear gods, let it not rain.

* * *

Jennie Treverton is a former newspaper journalist based in Treorchy, Wales, currently studying for a PhD in Ancient History. Her research is driven by an interest in lived experience in antiquity, among all levels of societies but particularly the Roman non-elite, women, and outsiders. In previous years she has had various pieces of short fiction published in the erotica genre, including under the Black Lace imprint. Today she writes historical fiction as a way of exploring how stories can illuminate lived realities past and present. Jennie has two children and in her spare time enjoys spending time in the mountains around her home in the South Wales Valleys.

HISTORICAL POETRY

PETER BRIDGES

JONATHAN CHAN

RICHARD ELLIOTT MARTIN

W. BARRETT MUNN

JENNIFER O'NEILL PICKERING

ALBERT SCHLAHT

ODYSSEUS AND THE PRINCESS

By Peter Bridges

Strong rowers brought our slim black vessel west
In just three days across a peaceful sea;
I happily saw high Scheria loom ahead
And hoped I had not come too late.

A shepherd on the shore saw us approach
And ran to tell the palace. Who could these strangers be,
Abroad in a time when good folk stayed at home
Harvesting and battening down for winter?

As we rowed slow into the port
I saw Alcinous there, with men black-cloaked for war
And more quick joining them from town.
I stood on the prow and called out to the king,
My faithful son Telemachus beside me,
Till finally tall Alcinous discerned in me his friend
Who'd gone, all thought, forever from Phaeacia.

I thought then of that recent day in Ithaca,
The path I took impatient through our mountain oaks
To reach the hut of Eumaeus,
My swineherd and my friend. I rested there
And asked him for the news of many years,
The years I'd spent away at bloody Troy.
Bad news, he said, but let Telemachus tell the tale;
He's coming soon for meat for the palace table.

Telemachus came and we embraced, and wept.
He'd grown to be a fine strong prince, I saw with pride;
But what could he tell me of our kingdom and my queen?

Alas, he said, my mother's dead; fine Queen Penelope is gone.
How so, how so? I pressed him and he told me all:
A pride of princely suitors'd sought her hand
When I had not returned and must be down in Hell.
Yet she'd refused them all, although they spent long months
Carousing and belligerent in my own marble halls.
They finally fell to fighting for the hand of my dear wife.
Some died; a few went back to their own petty princedoms.
One night the prince Eurymachus rushed her in her room;
She was surprised, but pulled a hidden knife;
But he too had a knife, and turned on her
And she fell sad and dead upon the floor.
That made Telemachus the king—but now came I.
So what to do? I'm sad, but glad for you, I said. Let no one know

Odysseus is alive, and you stay monarch all the years to come;
Just ready me a ship to take this old traveler
A few days down the sea to the kingdom I'd reached half-dead
To win their king's respect and the love of his sweet daughter.

I'd yearned to stay in Ithaca, my land, with wife and son;
But poor Penelope was dead. I would go on, for bad or good,
And future folk might weave tall tales of old Odysseus
And carnage he, not puling princes, wreaked in Ithaca.

We sailed, then, soon into a rosy dawn
After two nights as a guest in my own high-roofed halls
And an hour's slow stroll in my queen's well-loved gardens
Where the autumn leaves were falling, golden emblems of her death.

At Scheria the king embraced me on the quay;
Tall true Alcinous said quickly I must stay;
He'd' want my wisdom, and my sword as well.
He greeted then my son, new king,
Who in an hour cast off for Ithaca—for Ithaca!—
And I, old exile, was an exile once again.

My thoughts were all on lovely Nausica*a*
.I feared to ask her father how she was—married, it might be.
Instead I said that I'd come back because my wife had died
And I would not contest my son's hold on our throne.

You're widowed? said Alcinous,
Then I will wed you to my lovely white-armed daughter,
Who's grieved long days since you've been gone,
And says she'll never take another.

My heart, still ardent, leaped in my aging breast.
I found her by the flowers and sweet trees of her gardens.
We sat beneath a bower in warm October sun.
Her hair and face shone out like some good goddess.
I looked in her gray eyes and knew I saw true love.

When evening came I met again Arete, gracious queen.
We feasted, drank the fine red wine,
And watched royal dancers daring complex steps;

But beyond welcome thoughts of a wedding
Alcinous seemed concerned, seemed worried;
Was some neighbor island bent on war?
Odysseus looked at the king and wondered,
His sword still sharp and ready for new battle.

His pretty princess, though, sat happy at her hero's side
Hoping the gods would give them years of bliss,
No storms at sea but feasts in country groves,
Never dread famines, but rich harvests of red fruit,
No strife, but noble sons and daughters
To guide the good land in wisdom and in peace.

Above, owl-eyed Athena smiled, and even dread Poseidon
Laid down for now his fearsome trident.

* * *

Peter Bridges received degrees from Dartmouth and Columbia. He spent three decades in the Foreign Service, much of it in the Mediterranean, and ended as ambassador to Somalia. Kent State University Press published his diplomatic memoir and the biographies of two notorious Americans, John Moncure Daniel and Donn Piatt. He recently self-published a memoir of his climbs, treks, and voyages. His poems and prose have appeared in *Copperfield Review*, *Eclectica Magazine*, *Michigan Quarterly Review*, *Virginia Quarterly Review*, and elsewhere.

SOHN KEE-CHUNG TO JESSE OWENS

By Jonathan Chan

Berlin, Germany, 1936

you ran for justice, i ran for shame.

your feet were light, you ran on clouds,
i ran, bogged down, by stones and sand.

i grasped your hand tight though your country would not,
that toothbrush moustache would spare you a wave.

i clutched an oak to cover my chest,
and waved their bloodstained hands away.

they called your name and sang your song,
i hung my head when they announced the wrong son.

your victory wore thin, by brittle white skin;
mine learned to breathe, again and again,

but no one could stop us from
running.

* * *

Jonathan Chan is a writer, editor, and graduate student at Yale University. Born in New York to a Malaysian father and South Korean mother, he was raised in Singapore and educated in Cambridge, England. He is interested in questions of faith, identity, and creative expression. He has recently been moved by the writing of Don Mee Choi, Boey Kim Cheng, and Henri Nouwen.

PHILLIS WHEATLEY LAUDS THE ROMAN LAUREL

By Deborah H. Doolittle

What fragrance this bay makes at break of day
when the somber and somnifacient shades
of night do fade away. What small wisdom
contained within this brew, remnants of what
all the celebrated Romans once knew,

when they Apollo-like bestrode golden
chariots down Roman roads past endless
archways of aqueducts and unbroken
columns of colonnades, I chose. Sweet bay,
if I may, I would inscribe leaf by leaf

my life's glory and weave a wreath, much like
the one that the famed Daphne wore, running
in the forest to evade the hunters
who pursued her like a mythical deer,
but this one for myself and my own story.

* * *

Deborah H. Doolittle has lived in lots of different places but now calls North Carolina home. A Pushcart Prize nominee, she is the author of *Floribunda* (Main Street Rag) and three chapbooks, *No Crazy Notions* (Birch Brook Press), *That Echo* (Longleaf Press), and *Bogbound* (forthcoming from Orchard Street Press). Some of her poems have recently appeared (or will soon appear) in *Collateral*, *Dark Moon Lilith*, *Evening Street Review*, *Exit 13*, *The Journal* (Wales), *Kakalak*, *The Kerf*, and in audio format on *The Writer's Almanac*. She shares a home with her husband, four housecats, and a backyard full of birds.

CEDAR MOUNTAIN

By Richard Elliott Martin

The woman is in black mourning dress,
her head in her hands, she fears the worst
has befallen her, her husband,
gone nearly a year, said he would return
he has not broken a promise
in the thirty years they've been married.
There has been no word, since the battle at Manassas.
Her family has gathered at a table,
son, wife, daughter, sister,
have escaped the Yankees.

The son is thinking of joining the army,
his family loathing the moment
he tells them he will go.
Worn from his labors, his farm, his homestead,
are scraping through the planting season,
awaiting the harvest, and praying
the War will not return.
Fields destroyed by marching men,
armies have plundered the family's meager crops.

His young daughter has prepared a meal,
her mother, father, aunt, sister
gathered in Sunday dress,
just after morning worship
on a bright August Sabbath.
She stands to serve, her movements smooth,
bright blue dress against the summer sky,
basket on the table giving way to
cornmeal, bread, fresh butter, smoked beef,
the order of the day.

* * *

Richard Elliott Martin, a native of Roanoke, Virginia, is a recent graduate of Virginia Commonwealth University in Richmond where he studied history and creative writing. He lives in Richmond.

THE BLACK DEATH

By W. Barrett Munn

The Black Death, not a rat brung it, but fleas
that. Fleas, I say, miserable creatures
misery in their wake and sailin' with us.

Keep a clean bunk they says, Oh, Aye, and who
has time for a clean bunk, Sir? Rats, and fleas.
Not I. Ship is my home, my length, my width,
tacking windward carryin' along Black Death

The first mate knows when he's sailin' with risk
there's danger signs in winds and seas, but we're
bringin' a cruel fate to an innocent
land with our hold filled with Black Tragedy.

* * *

W. Barrett Munn is a retired registered nurse who lives with his wife Shelia in Tulsa, OK. He has previously had success writing stories with young protagonists that were published in magazines for both adults and children such as *Child Life*.

ARTEMESIA

By Jennifer O'Neill Pickering

My mother is born in
a time of rebirth
named after
the moon goddess,
huntress of the woods
twin to Apollo.

In an apprenticeship of boys,
is a father's favorite,
studies Caravaggio,
masters chiaroscuro,
describes the delicacy of Tuscan light,
is chemist of Hematite and Ochre.

Like her sister artists.
Lavinia, Diana, Elisabetta,
does not embroider pillows
royalty kneel upon.

She births, images of the Madonna,
the one called the Messiah,
paints stories of women from myth and Bible;
Susanna e i Vecchioni
Giuditta che decapita Oloferne
and though tears are a good binder
sweat is better.

Wed to the brush,
possessed by a steady hand,
sketches under paintings,
burns with passion,
raises five children,
divorces one husband,
is gifted beyond her womb
scorned by clergy is
caned by righteousness.

Pregnant with imagination
wears smocks
stained in linseed oil,
scaffolds her way to heaven,
signs her name to canvases
from Florence to Rome.

Though she's told since childhood,
women are of Adam's rib,
she is not broken.

or forgotten.

* * *

Jennifer O'Neill Pickering's new poetry book, *Fruit Box Castles: Poems from a Peach Rancher's Daughter* is available from Finishing Line Press. She is a Pushcart Nominee for Poetry and a finalist in the New Women's Voices Chapbook Competition. Her short story, "Summer of the River Bottom Dragon" is featured in PenDust Radio. Her poetry and prose appear across the country in *The Arlington Literary Journal, The Dog with the Old Soul, Raven's Perch, Restore and Restory: A Peoples History of the Cache Creek Nature Preserve, Poydras Review, Voices Project,* and elsewhere. Her poem "I Am the Creek" was selected for the site-specific sculpture Open Circle, an art in public places project in Sacramento, CA. She is a literary and visual artist who has taught art at college as well as in public and private settings, including a homeless shelter. Jennifer is a Board Member Emeritus of the Sacramento Poetry Center.

OCTOBER 3, 1873

By Albert Schlaht

the day Kintpuash and his followers
left this world to be with their ancestors

hang 'em, He said—
    because they sought to live on ancient land,
    because they fought to retain in their hands,

that which white settlers most greedily sought
and the Army for them brazenly fought—

hang 'em, He said

* * *

Albert Schlaht, a native of Big Sky Country, resides in the Rocky Mountains, home of the University of Montana, where he received his degree in Creative Writing. His first book, *The Schlaht Family History*, was released in 2007, followed by a book of poetry, *Singers in the Skull*. Several of his poems have appeared in *Presence, Shamrock Haiku Journal, Copperfield Review, Scifaikuest, Haiku Corner*, and other publications.

BOOK REVIEW:

THE LIGHT OF DAYS

REVIEW BY BRIANA BEEBE

The Light of Days: The Untold Story of Women Resistance Fighters in Hitler's Ghettos
Written by Judy Batalion
WILLIAM MORROW & CO, 2022
558 pp. Price: $ 28.99

Judy Batalion's *The Light of Days* recounts the seldom-told stories of female resistance fighters in the Holocaust, illuminating their fortitude and grit in face of calamity. Throughout this historical nonfiction, Batalion is able to bring this group of young female resistance fighters out of obscurity and into the light.

The story follows Renia Kukielka, a fourteen-year-old girl at the time of Hitler's first invasion of Poland in 1939. Renia risks her life for her culture: "Like so many Jewish women across the country, she did not think of herself as a political person...yet here she was, risking her life in action" (59). Renia and the rest of the young resistance fighters used this epiphany to take their fate, and the fate of other Jewish people, into their own hands. Batalion reveals how these passionate, courageous teenagers aided countless Jewish people in their collective fight for survival in Nazi Germany. It is refreshing to read historical nonfiction devoted to the strength of women in World War II and how their collective efforts transformed the outcomes of the war.

As Renia attempts to smuggle herself and another young girl to Warsaw with fake documentation, she is thrown in prison and punished by Nazis. But even in the face of excruciating pain, Renia exhibits vigor, "Now the lashes struck not just her back but her entire body-- face, neck, legs. She became weaker and weaker, but still Renia didn't speak. She would not show frailty. She would not" (338). Renia has unmatched grit, a spirit so full of hope that she is able to take part in an influential resistance movement as a young adult. Renia and her fellow fighters know that it is easier to give up, to shut down, to hide, to take flight. Instead, they show unimaginable strength. *The Light of Days*' feminine focus is a heartbreakingly beautiful success, and I commend Batalion's portrayal of heroic women.

Reading this account begs the question: if these individuals were able to do this in their time, what can I do in mine? Reading about the significance of such heroic actions elevates one's ideas of what humans can achieve. Thanks to Judy Batalion, the daring determination, fiery passion, and kind hearts of the "Ghetto Girls" will never be forgotten.

* * *

Briana Beebe is a sophomore studying Creative Writing and Literature at Eckerd College in St. Petersburg, Florida. In 2021, she was awarded the Melnick Scholarship for Creative Writing and recognized as a Peter Pav scholar. Though Briana is content with reviewing books for now, she hopes to write her own someday.

IDEAS FOR MARKETING HISTORICAL FICTION

BY SALLY R. RAE

As I've been getting ready to publish the first books in my Regency romance series, *The Duke's Daughters*, I've started to do some research about ways I can market my historical romances. Of course, I'm writing my books because I love to write, but I also want Regency readers to find my stories and enjoy them. Here are a few of the top tips for marketing historical fiction that I've found helpful and I hope you find them helpful too.

1. **Paid Advertisements.** BookBub is the main advertising site, but it can be difficult to land a spot with them. If you have a book out, you can certainly try for a BookBub ad. Who knows? Your book might land a coveted spot. There are also other book advertising sites such as The Fussy Librarian and FreeBooksy. The important point to remember is that your book needs to be on sale in order to advertise. The general consensus is that books prices at free or 99 cents do better because readers subscribed to these lists are looking for bargains. As the author, you may not make much money from your sales, but at the beginning of our writing careers, I think it's more important to develop a readership than it is to make a profit. The profit will come later if we take the time to cultivate relationships with readers.

2. **Cost Per Click Advertisements.** This is another form of advertising that you can find on Facebook, Amazon, and BookBub. You set up your advertising campaign, decide how much you want to spend over how many days, and you can tailor your ad so that it appears to readers who might be interested in your type of book.

3. **Social Media.** I've heard that BookTok is all the rage these days, and Instagram is also supposed to be good for getting attention for books. I gave up social media when I left my media job, so I'm going to have to learn the ins and outs all over again. Frankly, I've never looked at TikTok, but my sons love it so maybe they can give their mother some pointers. Tweeting "Buy my book!" doesn't work anymore, if it ever worked. I received a lot of tweets like that when I was a journalist and I looked right past them and even unfollowed accounts who kept spamming me with their book ads. Social media does take time and commitment, so if that's something you're interested in I suggest reading a bit about how to successfully build an audience. Don't forget that each platform requires something different, so that's a new learning curve for each platform you want to use.

4. **Perma-Free First in Series.** My author friends talk about this marketing tip with mixed emotions. Some authors swear by the free first in series tactic and others loathe the idea because the thought of giving their books away without making any money in return is too difficult for them to grasp. This is something I'm going to try. I'm finishing up the first three books in my Regency romance series and I'm going to release them together so I can make the first book free. The logic is that if someone takes a chance on a new author like me with a free book, and if they like that free book, then they're more willing to pay for the subsequent books. Of course, you need to have more than one book out in order to make this possible. That's why I held off publishing the first two books in my series--so I could put the first three out together. I know how much work and time it takes to write a book, and I know the thought of giving that work away for free can be painful, but I refer you back to my earlier point that at the beginning of our careers it's more important to find readers. If luring new readers to my books with a freebie helps, I'm all for it.

5. Local Media. I know everyone wants to be on the big national media channels, but as a former journalist, I can tell you that you can make a bigger splash locally because those are the people who will be interested in what you have to say. Regional journalists are always looking for interesting stories about local citizens. You don't want to blindly send out generic press releases that are just about your book. Those are a dime a dozen and there's nothing newsworthy in a new book release. I never gave such press releases a second glance. But if you can find an interesting angle that makes you the center of a great story, I would bet that you can find a local journalist who's interested. Search for local newspapers, magazines, and public access television stations and make your case. You don't need a publicist to do this for you. It will take some time, but you can find journalists' names and email addresses in their publications.

A friend of mine who has been publishing for several years recently told me that it's harder to get your books noticed these days because there are so many books available. I'm not sure if that's true, but even if it is, there are still proactive things we can do to help get our novels the attention they deserve. I believe in the concept of trial and error. Some things I try will work and others won't. I'll keep trying because I want my books to be read, and I bet you do too.

* * *

Sally R. Rae is a former journalist from Florida who has found her second wind as a writer of Regency-style romances in the tradition of Georgette Heyer. She has a double degree in Journalism and English from Florida State University. She lives with her husband, two children, and three dogs in Fort Lauderdale.

COPPERFIELD REVIEW QUARTERLY'S

Call For Submissions

The Copperfield Review/CRQ is now accepting article, book review, and author interview proposals. We will begin publishing our new feature columns in our Autumn edition, which will appear on October 31, 2022.

To submit a proposal for an article, book review, or an author interview, send a 200-word query stating your idea for your article, your reason for writing it, and a brief (up to 200 words) example of your writing to **submitcopperfield@gmail.com**. Proposals should be sent as Word files. Proposals sent as Google docs links will not be read. We do not accept simultaneous submissions for articles, books reviews, or author interviews. Authors can expect a response to their proposals in 6-12 weeks.

If we choose to commission a full-length article from you, the article should be 1000-1500 words long. Author interviews should be at least 1500-words long. Interviews should be with authors of historical fiction or history-based nonfiction. Sometimes we may commission shorter articles based on the needs of CRQ at that time.

Keep in mind that *The Copperfield Review* is a journal of historical fiction. We are interested in articles that relate to creativity, writing historical fiction, researching historical fiction, and living a creative life, as well as publishing and marketing historical fiction. We are interested in book reviews of historical novels published within the last 12 months. We are also interested in how writers handle the challenges of remaining creative despite the demands of daily life. We are not interested in history-based or academic nonfiction.

Historical fiction and history-based poetry are still submitted using our Submittable page, which can be found on copperfieldreview.com or copperfieldreviewquarterly.com.

We are excited about expanding *The Copperfield Review* and we look forward to your submissions.